# WAR AND PEACE

*Leo Tolstoy*

Spark Publishing
A Division of Barnes & Noble
120 Fifth Avenue
New York, NY 10011
www.sparknotes.com

ISBN-13: 978-1-5866-3814-6
ISBN-10: 1-5866-3814-9

Please submit changes or report errors to www.sparknotes.com/errors.

Printed and bound in the United States

5   7   9   10   8   6

# INTRODUCTION: STOPPING TO BUY SPARKNOTES ON A SNOWY EVENING

Whose words these are you *think* you know.
Your paper's due tomorrow, though;
We're glad to see you stopping here
To get some help before you go.

Lost your course? You'll find it here.
Face tests and essays without fear.
Between the words, good grades at stake:
Get great results throughout the year.

Once school bells caused your heart to quake
As teachers circled each mistake.
Use SparkNotes and no longer weep,
Ace every single test you take.

Yes, books are lovely, dark, and deep,
But only what you grasp you keep,
With hours to go before you sleep,
With hours to go before you sleep.

# Contents

# CONTEXT

L EV (LEO) NIKOLAEVICH TOLSTOY WAS BORN into a large and wealthy Russian landowning family in 1828, on the family estate of Yasnaya Polyana. Tolstoy's mother died when he was only two years old, and he idealized her memory throughout his life. Indeed, many critics believe that the angelic Princess Mary in *War and Peace* is modeled on this idealized memory of the author's mother. The family moved to Moscow when Tolstoy was nine. Shortly afterward, his father was murdered while traveling. Being orphaned before the age of ten, albeit without financial worries, left Tolstoy with an acute awareness of the power of death—an idea central to all his great works.

Though an intelligent child, Tolstoy had little interest in academics. His aunt had to work hard to persuade him to go to university, and he failed his entrance exam on his first attempt. Eventually, at the age of sixteen, Tolstoy matriculated at Kazan University. He studied law and Oriental languages, showing an interest in the grand heroic cultures of Persia, Turkey, and the Caucasus that persisted throughout his life. He was not popular at the university, and was very self-conscious about his large nose and thick eyebrows. Ultimately, Tolstoy was dissatisfied with his education, and he left the university in 1847, without a degree.

In 1851, Tolstoy visited his brother in the Russian army and then decided to enlist himself shortly afterward. He served in the Crimean War (1854–1856) and recorded his experience in his *Sevastopol Stories* (1855), in which he.developed techniques of representing military actions and deaths that he would later use in *War and Peace*. During his time in the army, Tolstoy produced a well-received autobiographical novel, *Childhood* (1852), followed by two others, *Boyhood* (1854) and *Youth* (1857).

In 1862, Tolstoy married Sofya Andreevna Behrs. He devoted most of the next two decades to raising a large family, managing his estate, and writing his two greatest novels, *War and Peace* (1865–1869) and *Anna Karenina* (1875–1877). In the years just prior to his marriage, Tolstoy had visited western Europe, partly to observe educational methods abroad. Upon returning, he founded and taught at schools for his peasants. His contact with his own peasants led to a heightened appreciation of their morality, camaraderie, and enjoyment of life, as evidenced in his celebration of Platon Karataev in *War and Peace*. Indeed, Tolstoy became quite critical of the superficiality of upper class Russians, as we can sense in his portraits of the Kuragin family in *War and Peace*. Ultimately, Tolstoy developed a desire to seek spiritual regeneration by renouncing his family's possessions, much to the dismay of his long-suffering wife.

Tolstoy's life spanned a period of intense development for Russia. The country was transformed from a backward agricultural economy into a major industrialized world power by the time of Tolstoy's death in 1910. This period witnessed major debates between two intellectual groups in Russia: the Slavophiles, who believed Russian culture and institutions to be exceptional and superior to European culture, and the Westernizers, who believed that Russia needed to follow more liberal, Western modes of thought and government. We see traces of this debate about the destiny of Russia—whether it should join Europe in its march toward secular values and scientific thought, or reject modernization and cherish the traditional, Asiatic elements of its culture—in Nicholas Rostov's dismissal of modern Western farming techniques in *War and Peace* and his distinctly Russian style of land management. We also see this debate in the novel's contrast between the logical Western mind of the arrogant Napoleon and the more holistic and humanitarian Russian minds of Pierre and Kutuzov. During this time, Russia was also undergoing a crisis of political thought, with a series of authoritarian tsars provoking liberal and radical intellectuals who demanded European constitutional rights—or even revolution—in Russia. Tolstoy's critical portrayal of leadership in *War and Peace* owes much to the Russian liberals' attack on authoritarian politics.

Tolstoy's turn to religion in his own life left an imprint on all his later writings. Works such as *A Confession* (1882) and *The Kingdom of God Is Within You* (1893) focused on the biblical Gospels' ideals of brotherly love and nonresistance to evil. The character of Pierre in *War and Peace* illustrates Tolstoy's moral commitment to humanity in a way that transcends class and nationality. Developing a reputation as a prophet of social thought, Tolstoy attracted disciples who came to his estate at Yasnaya Polyana seeking out his wisdom.

In 1898, Tolstoy published a radical essay called *What Is Art?*, in which he argued that the sole aim of great art must be moral instruction, and that on these grounds Shakespeare's plays and even Tolstoy's own novels are artistic failures. Increasingly frustrated by the disparity between his personal moral philosophy and his wealth,

and by his frequent quarrels with his wife, Tolstoy secretly left home in November 1910, at the age of eighty-two. He fell ill with pneumonia during his travels and died several days later in a faraway railway station. Tolstoy was mourned by admirers and followers around the world, and to this day is regarded as one of the greatest novelists in history.

## A NOTE ON RUSSIAN NAMES

To English-speaking readers, the names of the characters in *War and Peace* may be somewhat confusing, as there are a number of name-related conventions in Russian that do not exist in English.

Each Russian has a first name, a patronymic, and a surname. A person's patronymic consists of his or her father's first name accompanied by a suffix meaning "son of" or "daughter of." Hence, Princess Drubetskaya is addressed as Anna Mikhaylovna (daughter of Mikhail), Count Bezukhov is called Kyril Vladimirovich (son of Vladimir), and so on. Characters in the novel frequently address each other in this formal manner, using both the first name and patronymic.

When characters do not address each other formally, they may use informal nicknames, or diminutives. Sometimes, these nicknames bear little resemblance to the characters' full names. For instance, Nicholas is sometimes called Kolya (the standard nickname for Nicholas or Nikolai); Natasha is sometimes called Natalya (her full name, for which Natasha is the diminutive).

Furthermore, surnames in Russian take on both masculine and feminine forms. In *War and Peace,* for instance, Andrew's surname is Bolkonski, while his sister Mary's surname takes the feminine form, Bolkonskaya. Likewise, Count Rostov is married to Countess Rostova, and their sons have the surname Rostov while their daughters have the surname Rostova.

Keeping these conventions in mind helps to distinguish characters as they are addressed by different names throughout the novel. However, the use of these conventions varies in different editions of *War and Peace,* as some translators choose to simplify or eliminate name variants in order to make the novel more accessible to an English-speaking audience.

# Plot Overview

War and peace opens in the Russian city of St. Petersburg in 1805, as Napoleon's conquest of western Europe is just beginning to stir fears in Russia. Many of the novel's characters are introduced at a society hostess's party, among them Pierre Bezukhov, the socially awkward but likeable illegitimate son of a rich count, and Andrew Bolkonski, the intelligent and ambitious son of a retired military commander. We also meet the sneaky and shallow Kuragin family, including the wily father Vasili, the fortune-hunter son Anatole, and the ravishing daughter Helene. We are introduced to the Rostovs, a noble Moscow family, including the lively daughter Natasha, the quiet cousin Sonya, and the impetuous son Nicholas, who has just joined the army led by the old General Kutuzov.

The Russian troops are mobilized in alliance with the Austrian empire, which is currently resisting Napoleon's onslaught. Both Andrew and Nicholas go to the front. Andrew is wounded at the Battle of Austerlitz, and though he survives, he is long presumed dead. Pierre is made sole heir of his father's fortune and marries Helene Kuragina in a daze. Helene cheats on Pierre, and he challenges her seducer to a duel in which Pierre nearly kills the man.

Andrew's wife, Lise, gives birth to a son just as Andrew arrives home to his estate, much to the shock of his family. Lise dies in childbirth, leaving Andrew's devout sister Mary to raise the son. Meanwhile, Pierre, disillusioned by married life, leaves his wife and becomes involved with the spiritual practice of Freemasonry. He attempts to apply the practice's teachings to his estate management, and share these teachings with his skeptical friend Andrew, who is doing work to help reform the Russian government.

Meanwhile, the Rostov family's fortunes are failing, thanks in part to Nicholas's gambling debts. The Rostovs consider selling their beloved family estate, Otradnoe. Nicholas is encouraged to marry a rich heiress, despite his earlier promise to marry Sonya. Nicholas's army career continues, and he witnesses the great peace between Napoleon and Tsar Alexander. Natasha grows up, attends her first ball, and falls in love with various men before becoming seriously attached to Andrew. Andrew's father objects to the marriage, and

4

requires Andrew to wait a year before wedding Natasha. Natasha reluctantly submits to this demand, and Andrew goes off to travel.

After Andrew departs, his father becomes irritable and cruel toward Mary, who accepts the cruelty with Christian forgiveness. Natasha is attracted to Anatole Kuragin, who confesses his love. She eventually decides that she loves Anatole and plans to elope with him, but the plan fails. Andrew comes home and rejects Natasha for her involvement with Anatole. Pierre consoles Natasha and feels an attraction toward her. Natasha falls ill.

In 1812, Napoleon invades Russia, and Tsar Alexander reluctantly declares war. Andrew returns to active military service. Pierre observes Moscow's response to Napoleon's threat and develops a crazy sense that he has a mission to assassinate Napoleon. The French approach the Bolkonski estate, and Mary and the old Prince Bolkonski (Andrew's father) are advised to leave. The prince dies just as the French troops arrive. Mary, finally forced to leave her estate, finds the local peasants hostile. Nicholas happens to ride up and save Mary. Mary and Nicholas feel the stirrings of romance.

The Russians and French fight a decisive battle at Borodino, where the smaller Russian army inexplicably defeats the French forces, much to Napoleon's dismay. In St. Petersburg, life in the higher social circles continues almost unaffected by the occupation of Moscow. Helene seeks an annulment of her marriage with Anatole in order to marry a foreign prince. Distressed by this news, Pierre becomes deranged and flees his companions, wandering alone through Moscow.

Meanwhile, the Rostovs pack up their belongings, preparing to evacuate, but they abandon their possessions to convey wounded soldiers instead. Natasha's younger brother Petya enters the army. On the way out of the city, the Rostovs take along the wounded Andrew with them. Pierre, still wandering half-crazed in Moscow, sees widespread anarchy, looting, fire, and murder. Still obsessed with his mission of killing Napoleon, he saves a girl from a fire but is apprehended by the French authorities. Pierre witnesses the execution of several of his prison mates, and bonds with a wise peasant named Platon Karataev.

Nicholas's aunt tries to arrange a marriage between Nicholas and Mary, but Nicholas resists, remembering his commitment to Sonya. Mary visits the Rostovs to see the wounded Andrew, and Natasha and Mary grow closer. Andrew forgives Natasha, declaring his love for her before he dies. General Kutuzov leads the Russian troops back toward Moscow, which the French have finally abandoned after their defeat at Borodino. The French force the Russian prisoners of war, including Pierre, to march with them. On the way, Platon falls ill and is shot as a straggler. The Russians follow the retreating French, and small partisan fighting ensues. Petya is shot and killed.

Pierre, after being liberated from the French, falls ill for three months. Upon recovering, he realizes his love for Natasha, which she reciprocates. Pierre and Natasha are married in 1813 and eventually have four children. Natasha grows into a solid, frumpy Russian matron. Nicholas weds Mary, resolving his family's financial problems. He also rebuilds Mary's family's estate, which had been damaged in the war. Despite some tensions, Nicholas and Mary enjoy a happy family life.

# CHARACTER LIST

*Anna Pavlovna Scherer* A wealthy St. Petersburg society hostess
and matchmaker for the Kuragin family, whose party
in 1805 opens the novel.

*Pierre Bezukhov* The large-bodied, ungainly, and socially
awkward illegitimate son of an old Russian grandee.
Pierre, educated abroad, returns to Russia as a misfit.
His unexpected inheritance of a large fortune makes
him socially desirable. Pierre is ensnared by the
fortune-hunting Helene Kuragina, whose eventual
deception leaves him depressed and confused, spurring
a spiritual odyssey that spans the novel. Pierre
eventually marries Natasha Rostova.

*Andrew Bolkonski* The intelligent, disciplined, and ambitious
son of the retired military commander Prince
Bolkonski. Andrew is coldly analytical and resistant to
flights of emotion. Lonely after the death of his wife,
Lise, he falls in love with Natasha, but is unable to
forgive her momentary passion for Anatole.

*Lise Bolkonskaya* Andrew's angelic wife, who dies in childbirth.

*Prince Bolkonski* Andrew's father, a stodgy and old-fashioned
recluse who lives in the country after his retirement
from the army and subsequent retreat from social life.
The old prince, cynical about modern life, is stern and
sometimes cruel toward his daughter Mary. In the war
with Napoleon, he returns to active military service,
but dies as the French approach his estate.

*Mary Bolkonskaya* The lonely, plain, and long-suffering
daughter of Prince Bolkonski. Princess Mary cares for
her father, enduring his cruel treatment with Christian
forgiveness. In the end, Nicholas Rostov weds Mary
and saves her from an unhappy solitude.

*Mademoiselle Bourienne* The French companion of Princess Mary, who lives with her on the Bolkonski estate. Mademoiselle Bourienne becomes the object of the old prince's affections shortly before his death.

*Julie Karagina* Mary's friend and pen pal. Julie, an heiress, lives in Moscow and eventually marries Boris.

*Count Ilya Rostov* A loving, friendly, and financially carefree nobleman who lives with his large family at Otradnoe, their estate south of Moscow. The old count piles up debts through luxurious living, eventually depriving his children of their inheritance—a failing for which he seeks his children's forgiveness before he dies.

*Countess Natalya Rostova* Count Rostov's wife. The countess is as neglectful of money matters as her husband, maintaining standards of luxury that prove a burden to her son Nicholas when he supports her after the count's death. The death of her youngest son, Petya, deeply affects the countess, sinking her into a gloom from which she never again emerges.

*Natasha Rostova* The lively and irrepressible daughter of the Rostov family, who charms everyone she meets. Natasha falls in love with a series of men and then becomes seriously committed to Andrew, though she ruins the relationship by engaging in a brief tryst with Anatole Kuragin. Eventually, Natasha marries Pierre and becomes a stout, unkempt matron.

*Nicholas Rostov* The impetuous, eldest Rostov son, who joins the Russian forces in 1805 and spends much of the novel on the front. Nicholas accumulates gambling debts that become burdensome for his family. However, we see his commitment to his family upon his father's death, when he supports his mother and cousin Sonya on his meager salary while continuing to pay off the family's debts. Nicholas eventually marries the heiress Mary, saving his family from financial ruin.

*Sonya Rostova* The humble cousin of Natasha and Nicholas, who lives with the Rostovs as a ward. Sonya and Nicholas were childhood sweethearts, but as adults, Sonya generously gives up Nicholas so that he can marry a rich woman and save the Rostov finances.

*Petya Rostov* The youngest Rostov son, who begs to join the Russian army. Petya, who is close to Natasha and beloved by his mother, is killed in partisan fighting after the French begin their withdrawal from Moscow.

*Vera Rostova* The eldest Rostov daughter. Vera is a somewhat cold, unpleasant young woman, and her only proposal of marriage comes from the officer Berg, who is candid about his need for her dowry.

*Vasili Kuragin* An artificial and untrustworthy Russian nobleman, and a special friend of Anna Pavlovna. Vasili continually tries to maneuver his children into lucrative marriages.

*Anatole Kuragin* Vasili's roguish and spendthrift son, who is on the hunt for a rich wife. Anatole falls for Natasha Rostova at the opera, causing her rift with Andrew Bolkonski.

*Helene Kuragina* Vasili's cold, imperious, and beautiful daughter, who seduces Pierre into marriage, only to take up with another man immediately. Helene, though known in social circles as a witty woman, is actually stupid and shallow.

*Hippolyte Kuragin* The ugly and undistinguished brother of Helene and Anatole.

*Princess Anna Mikhaylovna Drubetskaya* A woman from an illustrious old family who is nonetheless impoverished. Anna Mikhaylovna is dominated by thoughts of securing a good future for her son Boris. She extracts a promise from Vasili Kuragin that he will help Boris get an officer's position in the army.

*Boris Drubetskoy* Anna Mikhaylovna's son, a poor but ambitious friend of Nicholas Rostov. Boris fights to establish a career for himself, using connections and his own intelligence and talents. Though he flirts with the young Natasha, as an adult he seeks a bigger fortune, eventually marrying an heiress.

*Dolokhov* A handsome Russian army officer and friend of Nicholas. Dolokhov carries on with Helene, prompting Pierre to challenge him to a duel in which Pierre nearly kills him.

*Denisov* A short, hairy, good-looking friend of Nicholas who accompanies him to Moscow on home leave and later falls for Sonya. Denisov is later court-martialed for seizing army food provisions to feed his men.

*Speranski* A brilliant liberal advisor to the tsar. Speranski attempts to reform and modernize the Russian state until his fall from grace.

*Bagration* A Russian military commander.

*General Kutuzov* An old, one-eyed general who leads the Russians to military success at Borodino, but who falls from favor toward the end of his life. Kutuzov is characterized by a spirituality and humility that contrast sharply with Napoleon's vanity and logic.

*Napoleon* The small, plump, and extremely arrogant French emperor and military leader who invades Russia. Napoleon embodies self-serving rationalization and vainglory in the novel, and he is shocked by the French defeat at Borodino.

# ANALYSIS OF MAJOR CHARACTERS

## PIERRE BEZUKHOV

Pierre, whom many critics regard as a reflection of Tolstoy himself, attracts our sympathy in his status as an outsider to the Russian upper classes. His simplicity and emotional directness contrast with the artificiality of fakes such as the Kuragins. Though the attendees at Anna Pavlovna's party consider Pierre uncouth and awkward, this very awkwardness emphasizes his natural unpretentiousness. We see his love of fun in his expulsion from St. Petersburg for excessive partying, and his generosity in his bank-breaking largesse toward friends and acquaintances following his inheritance. Pierre, though intelligent, is not dominated by reason, as his friend Andrew is. Pierre's emotional spurts occasionally get him into trouble, as when his sexual passions make him prey to the self-serving and beautiful Helene. His madcap escape into the city of Moscow and his subsequent obsessive belief that he is destined to be Napoleon's assassin show his submission to irrational impulses. Yet there is also a great nobility in Pierre's emotions, and his search for meaning in his life becomes a central theme of the novel. We feel that his final marriage to Natasha represents the culmination of a life of moral and spiritual questioning.

## ANDREW BOLKONSKI

Andrew, though as noble a soul as Pierre, differs from his friend in important ways that make him a very distinct character, and that illustrate Tolstoy's philosophy of life. Andrew has a highly intelligent and analytical mind, as we see in the profitable way he runs his estate. He is devoted to his country, returning to active duty even after nearly being killed at Austerlitz, and spending months helping Speranski write a new civil code for Russia. Andrew, though often detached, is emotionally honest and willing to examine mysteries in himself, as we see in his frank admission early in the novel that he is dissatisfied with marriage to his virtuous and lovely wife, Lise. But

Andrew's flaw is a spiritual one: his detachment is an intellectual advantage, but an emotional handicap. Andrew is free from Pierre's disabling search for the meaning of life, but he is also unable to forge deep and lasting connections with others, and unwilling to forgive their misdeeds. When Andrew is first introduced, Pierre touches his arm; Andrew instinctively flinches, disliking the contact. This physical reaction reflects Andrew's inability to be touched by others throughout his life. Ultimately, he is a lonely individual whom even the love of Natasha cannot save.

## NATASHA ROSTOVA

Natasha is one of Tolstoy's grandest creations, a representation of joyful vitality and the ability to experience life fully and boldly. The antithesis of Helene Kuragina, her eventual husband's first wife, Natasha is as lively and spontaneous as Helene is stony and scheming. From infancy to adulthood, Natasha charms everyone who meets her, from the guests of the Rostovs who witness her unintelligible comments about her doll, to Andrew Bolkonski, Anatole Kuragin, and finally Pierre Bezukhov. Yet, despite her charms, Natasha never comes across as a show-off or a flirt angling for men's attentions. Whether running in the fields in a yellow dress, singing on her balcony at Otradnoe, or simply sitting in an opera box, Natasha inspires desire simply by being herself, by existing in her own unique way. Her simplicity sometimes makes her naïve, however, as when she misunderstands her momentary passion for Anatole and makes absurd plans to elope with him. But Natasha repents her error with a sincerity that elicits forgiveness even from the wronged Andrew on his deathbed. Natasha's spiritual development is not as philosophical or bookish as Pierre's, but it is just as profound. She changes radically by the end of the novel, growing wise in a way that makes her Pierre's spiritual equal.

## GENERAL KUTUZOV

The commander of the Russian forces against Napoleon, Kutuzov is old, fat, and one-eyed—hardly the archetypal image of military leadership. Yet Kutuzov is a brilliant strategist as well as a practiced philosopher of human nature, and Tolstoy's respect for him is greater than for any other government functionary among the French or Russians—greater even than his respect for the somewhat oblivious Tsar Alexander. Kutuzov is humble and spiritual, in sharp contrast to the vain and self-absorbed Napoleon with his cold use of logic. After the Battle of Borodino, Kutuzov stops at a church procession and kneels in gratitude to a holy icon, demonstrating a humility of which Napoleon certainly would be incapable. Kutuzov is motivated by personal belief rather than the desire for acceptance, which makes his final fall from grace only a minor tragedy for him. Whereas Napoleon is always convinced of being absolutely right, Kutuzov is more realistic and wary about the state of things. He hesitates to declare a Russian victory at Borodino despite the obvious advantages of doing so, partly because the experiences of his long career have proved that reality is always more complex than one initially thinks. Such awareness of the mysteries of existence win Kutuzov our—and Tolstoy's—approval.

## PLATON KARATAEV

Though Platon Karataev makes only a brief appearance in a few chapters of this immense novel, he has won an admiration from readers and critics that has endured from the publication of *War and Peace* through the Soviet period and up to the present day. One of the few peasants in the novel to whom Tolstoy gives deep, individualized characterization, Platon represents the author's ideal of the simple, life-affirming philosophy of the Russian peasantry (Platon is the Russian name for Plato, the Greek philosopher). Platon lives in the moment, forgetful of the past and oblivious of the future, to the extent that he cannot even remember what he said a few minutes earlier. His affinity with animals, like the little dog accompanying the Russian political prisoners, suggests that he too lives by instinct rather than by reason. He spouts Russian proverbs that resound with wisdom. Overall, this characterization of an extraordinarily happy human being contrasts sharply with Pierre, who has been depressed and confused for dozens of chapters when he meets Platon. Platon thus appears as a kind of answer to Pierre's long spiritual questionings, living proof that the human search for contentment can be a successful one.

# THEMES, MOTIFS & SYMBOLS

## THEMES

*Themes are the fundamental and often universal ideas explored in a literary work.*

### THE IRRATIONALITY OF HUMAN MOTIVES

Although a large portion of *War and Peace* focuses on war, which is associated in our minds with clear-headed strategy and sensible reasoning, Tolstoy constantly emphasizes the irrational motives for human behavior in both peace and war. Wisdom is linked not to reason but to an acceptance of how mysterious our actions can be, even to ourselves. General Kutuzov emerges as a great leader not because he develops a logical plan and then demands that everyone follow it, but rather because he is willing to adapt to the flow of events and think on his feet. He revises his plan as each stage turns out to be vastly different from what was expected. Similarly irrational actions include Nicholas's sudden decision to wed Mary after previously resolving to go back to Sonya, and Natasha's surprising marriage to Pierre. Yet almost all the irrational actions we see in the novel turn out successfully, in accordance with instincts in human life that, for Tolstoy, lie far deeper than our reasoning minds.

### THE SEARCH FOR THE MEANING OF LIFE

Several characters in *War and Peace* experience sudden revelations about the absurdity of existence. Andrew, for instance, has a near-death experience at Austerlitz that shows him a glimpse of the truth behind the falsity of earthly life. While Andrew needs a brush with death to bring about this spiritual vision, Pierre spends most of the novel wondering why his life is so empty and artificial. The immediate cause of Pierre's philosophizing is his marriage to the wrong woman, but his pondering goes beyond Helene alone, to include the vast mystery of why humans are put on Earth. Pierre's involvement with the mystical practice of Freemasonry constitutes his attempt to give meaning to his life. Tolstoy, however, shows the inadequacies of this approach, as Pierre grows bored with the Masons and dissatisfied with their passivity. Pierre's involvement with politics, shown in his short-lived, crazy obsession with assassinating Napoleon, is equally shallow. What finally gives meaning to Pierre's life is the experience of real love with Natasha.

## THE LIMITS OF LEADERSHIP

Tolstoy explores characters on both the highest and lowest rungs of the social ladder in *War and Peace,* giving us realistic portraits of peasants and tsars, servants and emperors. Consequently, we not only get a close look at lofty leaders like Napoleon and Alexander, but also a chance to view them against the backdrop of society as a whole, an opportunity to assess these leaders' overall usefulness and role on a general level. In this regard, Tolstoy gives us a no-nonsense, democratic evaluation of princes, generals, and other supposed leaders—and the result is not very flattering. Nicholas's first glimpse of Alexander produces surprise at the fact that the tsar is just an ordinary man. Our view of Napoleon is even worse: when we see him in his bathroom getting his plump little body rubbed down, it is hard to imagine him as the grand conqueror of Europe. Tolstoy's philosophy of history justifies his cynicism toward leaders, for, in his view, history is not a creation of great men, but is rather the result of millions of individual chains of cause and effect too small to be analyzed independently. Even emperors, though they may imagine they rule the world, are caught in these chains of circumstance.

# MOTIFS

*Motifs are recurring structures, contrasts, or literary devices that can help to develop and inform the text's major themes.*

## INEXPLICABLE LOVE

*War and Peace* is full of romantic mate-choices made without a full grasp of their consequences, some of them with disastrous results. Pierre marries the beautiful Helene in a daze of sexual passion and naïve trust, and his life almost immediately becomes a constant torment as Helene cheats on him with his friend. Natasha is smitten with the rakish Anatole and prepares to elope with him without seeing that his irresponsible ways would bring her to misery. Her crush on Anatole costs her a chance with Andrew, who cannot forgive her lapse. In both cases, an unreasoned romantic impulse ends up being destructive. Yet Tolstoy does not condemn irrational love. The two great love stories that conclude the novel—between Natasha and Pierre and between Mary and Nicholas—both take their lovers, and us as readers, by surprise. It suddenly occurs to all of them that they are in love, despite having very different expectations in mind. Unexplained love can be a horrible mistake, but it can also be wonderful. At its best, unpredictable love is a symbol of the mysterious forces of human life and instinct that cannot be denied.

## FINANCIAL LOSS

The loss of substantial amounts of money or property is a recurrent motif throughout the novel, and is associated in particular with the Rostov family. The family's fortunes are already in decline at the beginning of the novel, as the irresponsible Count Rostov has dissipated his children's inheritance through careless spending. Nicholas's gambling losses accelerate the decline, and then the family is forced to abandon their Moscow home and most of their belongings as the French invade the city. But these financial losses are not necessarily signs of failure. Tolstoy, who himself gave away possessions in search of spiritual regeneration later in life, shows in *War and Peace* the positive side of the Rostovs' material misfortunes. Count Rostov's gracious payment of Nicholas's debts shows a powerful connection between father and son, a connection that Nicholas affirms by vowing to repay his debt in five years. His early financial losses appear to leave him wiser, and later in life he becomes a savvy landowner. Moreover, the Rostov spirit for life, unhindered by compromised finances, ends up breeding charismatic children who marry into two of the largest fortunes in Russia—that of the Bolkonskis and that of the Bezukhovs. In a sense, Tolstoy may even be hinting that financial carelessness has the capacity to ultimately produce a spiritual richness worth far more than the mere material wealth.

## DEATH AS A REVELATION

Death in *War and Peace* is never just a biological end, but almost always a moral event that brings some philosophical revelation. The first major instance of death as a revelation is Andrew's near-death experience at Austerlitz, when he lies on the field blissfully aware of how little the external world matters and rejoicing that its burden has been lifted from his shoulders. Andrew does not even care that Napoleon himself passes by and comments on him, as earthly values of rank and power have lost all their meaning to him. Tolstoy's portrayals of death's revelatory power also include epiphanies some characters experience upon the deaths of others. One example is Pierre's powerful reaction to the execution of the Russian prisoners of war in the French army camp, which leads him to radical thoughts on the insanity of war and the brotherhood of mankind. Pierre's reverence for the inspirational Platon makes the latter's execution prompt an existential crisis in Pierre. Similarly, Andrew's death leads Natasha to a profound change in her outlook, making her far more reflective and serious than ever before. Perhaps Natasha, without the experience of grieving for Andrew, would never become mature enough to marry Pierre in the end. In this sense, death is not merely the end of life, but a powerful lesson in faith and philosophy.

## Symbols

*Symbols are objects, characters, figures, or colors used to represent abstract ideas or concepts.*

### The Battle of Borodino

The Battle of Borodino is far more than a decisive military turning point in the clash between Napoleon and the Russians. Abundantly overlaid with Tolstoy's philosophy of history and free will, Borodino becomes a symbol of the conflict between two very different conceptions of human life and action. The French imagine that they obey reason and strategy in maneuvering troops and plotting battles, and they are confident that they will win because of their logical advantages, such as their superior manpower and supplies. The Russians, by contrast, follow more instinctive and less rational principles. They fight spiritually, with their whole beings, just as Kutuzov is said to lead them spiritually. When Kutuzov kneels before an icon after the Battle of Borodino, we see that faith, rather than reason, is his guiding light. Tolstoy depicts this spiritual victory at Borodino as a kind of minor miracle, inexplicable in rational terms—an event that, for Tolstoy, illustrates the superiority of Russian spirit to European reason.

## THE FRENCH OCCUPATION OF MOSCOW

On a basic level, the French occupation of Moscow is a tragic event in the history of the Napoleonic wars. Tolstoy, however, makes the occupation of the city into a symbol of the European cultural invasion of Russia, using it to criticize Russian dependency on foreign styles and institutions wrongly deemed superior to native ones. In cultural terms, the French takeover of Russia was underway long before Napoleon burst onto the historical scene. We see that the French-Russian conflict is a deep and complex one, as Tolstoy opens *War and Peace* with a conversation between two Russians chatting in French about their fears of a war with France. The threat is both external and internal, as the Russian nobility, in many ways, appears far closer to the French than to their own Russian peasantry. Though we hear of Prince Golitsyn taking Russian lessons to avoid speaking French, we sense that this measure will not be enough to give the Russian gentry a truly native cultural identity. Therefore, it is highly symbolic that Pierre—referred to using the French form of "Peter" rather than the Russian "Petr"—receives spiritual illumination not from a Western source, but from a home-grown Russian peasant, Platon Karataev. The answer to the French occupation of Russia, Tolstoy implies, lies in greater appreciation of native Russians like Platon.

## NICHOLAS'S REBUILDING OF BALD HILLS

At the end of the Napoleonic wars, Nicholas's finances are in ruins: his father is dead and has left huge debts, while his mother expects to live in the same luxury she has always enjoyed. Nicholas's Moscow home was left to French marauders, and it is doubtful whether anything of value will remain after the Rostovs return. Nicholas's marriage to the wealthy Mary Bolkonskaya, then, comes as a sweet relief—both an emotional and a financial regeneration. His rebuilding of Mary's family's old estate, Bald Hills, is symbolic not just of the restoration of his own financial well being, but of the continuing prosperity of the old Russian spirit. The Rostovs may have appeared to be in decline, but at the end of the novel they are stronger than ever, enriched by Natasha's Pierre and Nicholas's Mary. The old Russian aristocracy may be less grand than before—Nicholas rebuilds Bald Hills on a smaller scale and with simple peasant-made furniture—but at least the estate continues, as a symbol of the indomitable old Russian traditions.

# SUMMARY & ANALYSIS

## BOOK ONE

### BOOK ONE, CHAPTERS 1–3

> *"I warn you . . . if you still try to defend the infamies*
> *and horrors perpetrated by that Antichrist—I really*
> *believe he is Antichrist—I will have nothing more to*
> *do with you. . . ."*          (See QUOTATIONS, p. 68)

At a society party in St. Petersburg in 1805, Anna Pavlovna Scherer speaks to her old friend Prince Vasili Kuragin about the threat Napoleon presents to Russia. Anna, calling Napoleon the Antichrist, declares that Russia alone must save Europe. The prospect of war dominates the conversations at the party. But Anna also raises more personal issues, expressing esteem for Vasili's children—especially the beautiful Helene—with the exception of Anatole, a rogue. Vasili asks Anna to arrange a meeting between his son Anatole and Mary Bolkonskaya, the lonely daughter of Prince Bolkonski, a rich, reclusive, retired military commander.

Meanwhile, Helene Kuragina arrives at the party, as does Lise, Bolkonski's daughter-in-law, who is married to his military officer son, Andrew. Next to arrive is Pierre, the unpolished and ungainly son of Count Bezukhov, educated abroad and only recently returned to Russia. The ugly Hippolyte Kuragin, Helene's brother, is also present.

> *Pierre . . . watched [Andrew] with glad, affectionate*
> *eyes. . . . Andrew frowned again, expressing his*
> *annoyance with whoever was touching his arm.*
>                    (See QUOTATIONS, p. 69)

Andrew Bolkonski arrives at the party. Vasili Kuragin promises a promotion to Boris, the only son of a well-connected but impoverished old acquaintance, Princess Anna Mikhaylovna Drubetskaya. Pierre voices approval of the French Revolution. After the soiree, Pierre visits Andrew at his house, where they discuss the idea of perpetual peace advanced by one of Anna's guests. Pierre believes in

19

this possibility of peace, but he thinks that such peace must be spiritual rather than political. Andrew advises Pierre not to marry, saying that marriage wastes a man's sense of purpose and resolve—the same resolve demonstrated by Napoleon.

Later, Pierre visits his friend Anatole at his house near the barracks, where the drunken officers are carousing with a trained bear, and Anatole's friend Dolokhov is proving that he can drink a bottle of rum while precariously perched on the window ledge.

## BOOK ONE, CHAPTERS 4–13

> *This black-eyed, wide-mouthed girl, not pretty but full of life . . . ran to hide her flushed face in the lace of her mother's mantilla—not paying the least attention to her severe remark—and began to laugh.*
>
> (See QUOTATIONS, p. 70)

Anna Mikhaylovna has gone to Moscow, to the home of her wealthy relatives, the Rostovs. Both the Rostov mother and youngest daughter are celebrating their name day (the feast day of the Christian saint after whom the women are named). The guests discuss Pierre's uncouth lifestyle.

The thirteen-year-old Rostov daughter, Natasha, appears, carrying her doll. She is accompanied by other children, including her brother Nicholas; his friend Boris, Anna Mikhaylovna's son; and Sonya, Count Rostov's niece—all of whom live in the Rostov household. Nicholas states that he is joining the army out of a sense of vocation rather than a wish to accompany Boris, who has been made an officer. Natasha mischievously hides in order to watch a tearful exchange between Nicholas and Sonya, in which Nicholas begs forgiveness for flirting with Julie Karagina, one of the guests. When Boris appears, Natasha seeks a kiss from him and extracts a half-joking promise of marriage in four years. Countess Rostova makes her daughter Vera leave the room, so that she and Anna Mikhaylovna may discuss financial worries. Anna Mikhaylovna hopes that Boris's godfather, the ailing Count Cyril Bezukhov, will help Boris.

Anna Mikhaylovna and Boris visit his dying godfather, Cyril Bezukhov. They are greeted by Vasili Kuragin, who, due to Pierre's illegitimacy, is the current heir to the Bezukhov fortune. Vasili fears that Anna Mikhaylovna will be a rival fortune-seeker. Boris goes upstairs to see Pierre, who has been expelled from St. Petersburg for riotous conduct, and the two men discuss their lives and financial situations. Meanwhile, Countess Rostova asks her husband for money for Boris's military uniform.

The Rostovs entertain dinner guests, including an officer, Berg, and a woman, Marya Dmitrievna Akhrosimova, known for her bluntness. Marya Dmitrievna gives a name day present to Natasha, who is one of the very few people not afraid of Marya. Over dinner, the idealistic Nicholas blurts out that Russia must conquer or die. After dinner, Natasha seeks out Sonya to join the guests for music and finds Sonya crying from despair that her love for her cousin Nicholas will never be sanctified with marriage. Natasha reassures Sonya.

Meanwhile, Count Bezukhov has had a sixth stroke, with no hope of recovery. Vasili Kuragin informs another potential heir, the Princess Catherine Semenovna, that the count has written a letter asking the tsar to legitimize his bastard son, Pierre, making him full and direct heir to his large fortune. Vasili and Catherine try to destroy the letter, but Anna Mikhaylovna prevents them. Pierre shyly visits his father's room and sees the dying man, but leaves when his father dozes. The count dies.

### BOOK ONE, CHAPTERS 14–16
At Bald Hills, Prince Nicholas Bolkonski's estate outside Moscow, the prince lives in seclusion with his daughter, Mary, and her companion, Mademoiselle Bourienne. After a difficult geometry lesson, Mary reads a letter from her friend Julie Karagina, who misses Mary and is sad that Nicholas Rostov has left to join the war. Julie also informs Mary of Pierre's inheritance. Mary writes back, counseling Julie to remember Christian patience and forgiveness.

Mary's brother, Andrew Bolkonski, arrives at Bald Hills with his wife, Lise. Andrew tells Mary that he will be leaving for the war soon. Over dinner, the family and a guest, Michael Ivanovich, discuss the war. The old Prince Bolkonski is contemptuous of Napoleon, while Andrew asserts the French emperor's grandeur. Mary is astonished at her brother's failure to revere their father, and finds him much changed. Andrew admits to his father and his sister that he is unhappy in his marriage to Lise. Prince Nicholas sends his son off to war with a letter to General Kutuzov requesting favors for Andrew. Andrew bids farewell to his family and leaves.

## ANALYSIS: BOOK ONE

Tolstoy introduces us to the deep and complex relationship between the two words of his novel's title—war and peace—from the opening scene at Anna Pavlovna's party. We see immediately that even the seemingly peacetime activity of partying is actually quite warlike. Anna runs her soirée with a precise strategy, much like a general, knowing exactly when to attack and when to withdraw. Her words to Vasili are described as an attack, and Vasili calls himself her slave. Though these phrases may be only metaphors, they nonetheless refer to a power structure in Russian high society that is as steely and directed as a war machine. Indeed, we soon see how much strategy Vasili uses to secure fortunes for his shiftless children Anatole and Helene, and how Helene herself is a ruthless gold-digger behind her marble beauty.

It is clear that the people in the society of *War and Peace* are on the attack, out for conquest. Moreover, we sense that those characters who are too naïve to recognize this warlike dynamic—as Pierre soon proves to be—will be defeated and plundered. Marya Dmitrievna even describes little Natasha as a "Cossack" warrior, using an admiring tone that suggests that the world of the novel is a place in which being called a warrior is a compliment. The idea that humans are fighting for their survival, holding off the enemy however they can, is a dominant motif throughout *War and Peace,* and one that Tolstoy examines from several angles. While the author never approves of extreme tactics, such as the cold-blooded ruthlessness of Helene Kuragina, it is arguable that he views love—and all of life, for that matter—as a battlefield upon which some sort of fighting is always necessary.

Tolstoy's exploration of war in this novel also raises complicated issues about what it means to identify with one's nation. The threat of a French war against Russia reveals the irony of a cultural situation in which, even in peacetime, the French-speaking Russian aristocrats already seem at war with the common, native Russian-speaking population. The division among nations during the Napoleonic wars also points to a division within Russia itself even before war begins. We hear, for example, that Hippolyte Kuragin speaks Russian like a foreigner. We wonder what the war against France might mean to this Russian who speaks only French. The cultural divide within the Russian nation in peacetime could, perhaps, simply become more noticeable in wartime, making the Napoleonic war an internal as well as an external threat.

# BOOKS TWO–THREE

### BOOK TWO, CHAPTERS 1–5

In October 1805, the Russian army, led by General Kutuzov, is settled near Braunau in Austria, the home of their ally, the Archduke Ferdinand. The soldiers are clean and orderly despite holes in their boots. Pierre's friend Dolokhov, demoted to the ranks, is criticized for inappropriate clothing, and he becomes resentful. The one-eyed General Kutuzov inspects the troops accompanied by his adjutant, Andrew Bolkonski. Kutuzov promises Dolokhov a promotion should he distinguish himself in battle. In conference with the Austrian commander, Kutuzov insincerely expresses regret that the tsar has not ordered the Russian troops to join the Austrian forces. Bolkonski rebukes a Russian who jokes about a recent major Austrian defeat.

At the Russian hussar (light cavalry) camp near Braunau, Nicholas Rostov and his commanding officer, Denisov, enjoy leisure time until a fellow officer, Telyanin, steals Denisov's purse and Nicholas demands it back. Nicholas accuses Telyanin publicly, which earns Nicholas charges of insubordination from his superior. Nicholas refuses to apologize.

The Russian troops retreat over a river, pursued by the enemy. The military scene is chaotic. A Russian officer, Nesvitski, is nearly crushed on a bridge as the troops march over it, and he hears snatches of their various conversations. He does not recognize a cannonball when it splashes in the water. Orders are misunderstood. The Russian hussars, including Nicholas, succeed in burning the bridge under enemy fire, although three Russians are shot. The commanding officers somewhat selfishly weigh the lost lives against praise for the platoon.

### BOOK TWO, CHAPTERS 6–10

Despite rumors of Napoleon's retreat, the French troops are gaining ground against Kutuzov's beleaguered Russian forces. Andrew Bolkonski is sent to the Austrian government-in-exile with news of a recent Russian victory. Along the way he gives money to wounded soldiers and dreams of the battle. Disappointed that the Austrian Minister of War seems more affected by the death of Schmidt, an Austrian general, than by the Russian victory, Andrew then chats with his friend Bilibin, a highly regarded diplomat.

Andrew shares his astonishment that the blundering Austrians are not appreciating Kutuzov's victories. Andrew reflects that the recent victory is not significant compared to the loss of Vienna to the French. Bilibin speculates darkly about the fact that Austria is considering a separate peace with the French, though Andrew refuses to believe this rumor. Andrew and Bilibin's officer friends chat about women and Andrew's upcoming meeting with the Austrian emperor. The officers advise Andrew to praise the emperor's supply of provisions for the Russian army, even if he must lie in order to do so.

During the meeting, the emperor, pleased with Andrew's news, confers state honors upon him. Returning from official visits, Andrew is surprised to find that Napoleon is again pursuing the Russian troops. Bilibin advises Andrew to stay with him rather than heroically join his own army on the move. Andrew, however, staunchly remains faithful to his army. But when he watches the Russian soldiers on the road, rudely refusing right of way to a helpless doctor's wife, he muses that the army is a chaotic mob. Meeting with Kutuzov, Andrew expresses his wish to join the imperiled battalion commanded by Prince Bagration. Kutuzov warns that the battalion is doomed, but Andrew says that is exactly why his presence is needed there. Meanwhile, Kutuzov tricks the French commander Murat into believing a ploy, ultimately weakening the French and earning Murat a chastising letter from Napoleon.

### BOOK TWO, CHAPTERS 11–16

A battle looms. Andrew witnesses Dolokhov chatting and laughing with the enemy across the battle lines. Drinking vodka, the troops muse upon life and death. The battle begins. Andrew rides beside Prince Bagration, noting that Bagration reacts to news of events on the field as though he had planned for them to happen, and that his manner improves the morale of all who speak to him. The two men encounter many wounded soldiers at a site where a Russian detachment has been overwhelmed. The commanding officer begs Bagration to turn back, but Bagration refuses.

Meanwhile, in the hussar lines, Nicholas Rostov is awaiting his first battle impatiently. Suddenly he is unsure who the enemy is, and whether he is wounded, as he feels blood and is pinned down by his fallen horse. Nicholas sees the enemy approach and cannot believe that they would want to kill him, a person whom everyone likes. He awaits aid and dreams of home.

Dolokhov is wounded while capturing an enemy officer, and wishes to be remembered for his heroism. Andrew wanders among the wounded soldiers. One soldier asks for water and wonders whether he is to die like a dog. Andrew saves a captain named Tushin from wrongful accusations of incompetence Bagration has levied, but he is soured by the experience.

### BOOK THREE, CHAPTERS 1–5

Back in Moscow, Pierre finds his former critics suddenly friendly now that he has become the wealthy Count Bezukhov. He naïvely believes these sycophants to be sincere. Vasili Kuragin has taken Pierre in hand with the ulterior motive of marrying him to his daughter, Helene, and borrowing forty thousand rubles. Anna Pavlovna Scherer invites Pierre to a party and sings the praises of Helene, whose beauty overwhelms Pierre even though he is aware she is stupid. Over time, Pierre's infatuation with Helene deepens until he is convinced that marriage is inevitable. At Helene's name day party, Vasili convinces everyone, including the dazed Pierre himself, that Pierre and Helene are engaged. They are married shortly afterwards. Vasili sends Prince Nicholas Bolkonski word that he will soon visit with his son Anatole, his ulterior motive being to arrange a marriage with Mary, the prince's daughter. The prince disapproves of Vasili's character and becomes grumpy.

As the idea of courtship appears before her, Mary is plagued by religious concerns about her desires of the flesh. She is overwhelmed by Anatole's beauty and self-possession. The prince, not wanting his daughter to get married and leave him, doubts that Anatole is good enough for Mary. Anatole does, however, charm the women—Mary, Lise, and especially Mademoiselle Bourienne. The prince ultimately decides to give his daughter total freedom in choosing her husband. Finally, Mary decides to remain with her father, rejecting Anatole.

The Rostovs receive a letter from Nicholas, telling of his injuries and of his promotion to officer rank. The count and countess both weep, as does Sonya. The countess muses on Nicholas's growth from infancy to manhood.

### BOOK THREE, CHAPTERS 6–13

Meanwhile, back at the front, Nicholas enjoys a free existence, falling into debt and going to restaurants. He is joined by his friend Boris and by the officer Berg. Nicholas is a bit contemptuous of

Berg's diplomatic tendencies, as he prefers more blatant acts of heroism. Andrew joins Nicholas and the others, and Nicholas throws some thinly veiled insults at Andrew about being a distant officer far from the fray of battle. Later, the Austrian and Russian emperors review their troops together, with Tsar Alexander winning cheers from his men. Nicholas feels a wish to die for the tsar, and the men are inspired to fight valiantly.

The next day, Boris acts on Berg's advice and sets out to seek patronage from Andrew. Boris finally finds Andrew, who kindly agrees to talk to him about becoming an adjutant (a staff officer). It is announced that the Russian and Austrian strategists have decided to attack the French, and Boris feels elated that he is in such important company. Nicholas also is overjoyed at having been reviewed by the tsar, with whom he is so fascinated he almost seems to be in love. Talks with Napoleon are underway, and Andrew learns from the Russian emissary that Napoleon fears a large battle. The plan remains to attack the French at Austerlitz, though General Kutuzov fears defeat. At the council of war, the commanders disagree and hesitate. Nonetheless, Andrew relishes the glory that he feels will come. Riding on horseback that night, Nicholas dozes and thinks of Natasha, but he is awakened by shots nearby. It is clear that action will follow soon. The next morning, the Russian troops advance, blinded by a fog and unsure whether they are in the midst of the French.

Rostov's detachment is frustrated to learn that they are late, due to a mix-up over misunderstood orders. Unbeknownst to the Russians, the French forces are nearby—in fact, Napoleon himself expressionlessly watches the Russians take their position. The tsar reproaches Kutuzov for delaying the battle, but Kutuzov responds that a battle is more serious than an official parade, and that being late is not as important as being strong. Suddenly the French appear closer than expected, and Kutuzov is wounded in the cheek. Andrew is wounded by a French bludgeon, and he falls to the ground in an attitude of bliss and peace, thanking God that all falsehood is vanishing around him. Meanwhile, on the right flank, Bagration's troops, including Nicholas, have not started fighting yet. The charge begins, with Rostov in it. All but eighteen of the officers die in the attack. Boris rides up, but Nicholas rides away, seeking the tsar with a message. Confusion reigns. The possibility of defeat is too horrible for Nicholas to contemplate.

Nicholas, still searching for Kutuzov or the tsar in the village of Pratzen, is told that the tsar has been transported away wounded. Nicholas cannot believe it, and he hears conflicting reports. Despairing, he sees the dead in the fields. He is surprised to find the tsar alone in a field, but he is too shy to address him, so he rides on. Later, Nicholas comes back to find the tsar gone. The cannon fire continues, and more men fall. Meanwhile, Andrew, lying in Pratzen, is unsure where he is and delirious after receiving his wound. Napoleon rides by and comments on Andrew, but even this hardly affects him. When Napoleon later speaks to the Russian prisoners of war, he is courteous and complimentary toward Andrew.

---

## ANALYSIS: BOOKS TWO–THREE

Perhaps the foremost idea in these chapters is the disillusionment of idealists. Tolstoy emphatically underlines the split between the grand, noble, or romantic ideas characters hold about concepts such as national unity, war, and leadership, and the disappointing reality these characters experience later.

Tolstoy opens Book Two by continuing to deflate the grand notion of the unity of the Russian nation, deepening his exploration of the internal divisions within Russia that he had implied in Book One. We see a microcosm of these internal rifts in the barracks, as our first glimpse of a military conflict is not between Russians and Frenchmen, but among Russians themselves: the officer Telyanin steals a purse and Nicholas accuses him of thievery. We wonder about the strength of national unity if the Russians fight among themselves even on the battlefield. Similarly, when the first two Russian casualties are reported, there is talk of how the detachment may be awarded a medal, with no mention of mourning the fellow Russians who have fallen. Even the scene in which the officer Nesvitski is stuck on the bridge—blocked not by the enemy but by the movement of his own troops—hints that Russians can be their own worst enemies, perhaps even as much as the French are.

Disillusionment also occurs on the level of individual characters. Andrew starts off with high-minded notions of heroism, giving money to wounded soldiers from his own pocket, and believing that the Austrian commanders would appreciate the import of a Russian victory. But during his mission to the Austrian general, Andrew discovers that the Austrians greet news of Kutuzov's triumphs with little more than indifference, despite a series of Austrian blunders that should leave them very grateful for a Russian success. This sudden understanding that recognition and credit are not always given fairly marks the start of Andrew's initiation into the realities of war, the beginning of a deadened attitude that he never truly shakes throughout the rest of the novel.

Tolstoy uses the battle scenes in this section primarily to explore leadership, especially the fact that men who are revered as super-human heroes have the same mundane, everyday aspects as common men. Both the French and the Russian sides of the battle make certain men into myths. Anna Pavlovna has already referred to Napoleon as the "Antichrist," and here the French emperor exhibits a mythical aspect: our first image of Napoleon is of him standing immobile and expressionless, as if he were a statue rather than a living man. Tsar Alexander is revered in similarly transcendent ways, and Nicholas is amazed, when he finds the tsar standing alone in a field, that such a great figure could appear so ordinary. When the tsar hesitates in his review of the Russian troops, Nicholas is surprised, thinking that a great man never hesitates. This close proximity of high commanders to lowly infantrymen produces an environment in which great leadership appears especially valuable. Indeed, we see that a revered leader like Alexander can inspire his troops to acts of heroic self-sacrifice. However, that same proximity of the great and the lowly also has the potential to disillusion those in the rank and file, making them realize that their mythical heroes are, in many aspects, simply men just like themselves.

## BOOKS FOUR–FIVE

### BOOK FOUR, CHAPTERS 1–9

Later, in 1806, Nicholas and his friend Denisov visit the Rostov home in Moscow while they are on leave. Nicholas's family greets him with enthusiasm. He is reminded of his promise to marry Sonya, who is now sixteen and beautiful. Meanwhile, Natasha, now fifteen, declares she does not wish to marry Boris. Denisov creates a fine impression in the Rostov house, to Nicholas's surprise.

Nicholas enjoys the high life as an eligible Moscow bachelor, drifting a bit away from Sonya. Count Rostov arranges a dinner for Bagration at the English Club. The Rostovs plan to invite Pierre, and are informed that Pierre's wife, Helene, has been compromising her virtue with Dolokhov, to Pierre's great sadness. Muscovite society finds it difficult to accept that the Russians might be defeated. It is presumed that Andrew has died, leaving behind a pregnant wife.

Pierre looks unhappy during the party at the English Club, concerned about rumors of his wife's adulterous liaisons. A poet reads verses in honor of Bagration, who arrives looking much less grand than he appears on the battlefield. Drinks are poured, toasts are made, and Count Rostov weeps with emotion. When Dolokhov toasts beautiful women, Pierre takes it as an insult and challenges Dolokhov to a duel, taking Nicholas as his second. The next day in the woods, Pierre reconsiders, believing he has acted hastily. Nonetheless, the duel must continue. Pierre pulls the trigger and wounds Dolokhov severely, but is himself unhurt.

Pierre wrongly assumes that he has killed Dolokhov, and reflects that the death is ultimately due to his own original decision to marry Helene when he did not actually love her—a decision that led to a life of lies with a cold wife. Helene, hearing about the duel, accuses Pierre of being an idiot and exposing them both to ridicule. Pierre announces that they must separate, and Helene agrees on condition that she receive a part of his fortune. He erupts in violence, but later cedes his lands to her and departs alone for St. Petersburg.

At Bald Hills, Prince Bolkonski receives news from Kutuzov about the apparent death of his son Andrew. The news is given to Mary, but withheld from Andrew's widow, Lise, for fear of harming her unborn baby. Not long after, Lise reports feeling unwell, and the midwife is called. Lise lies waiting. Suddenly, a carriage is heard in the drive—it is Andrew, who appears to Mary on the landing of the staircase. He arrives as Lise is in labor. Soon after, Andrew's son is born, and his wife dies in childbirth.

## BOOK FOUR, CHAPTERS 10–15

In Moscow, Dolokhov convalesces and befriends Nicholas. At the Rostov home, everyone likes Dolokhov except Natasha, who sees him as a bad man. Dolokhov develops an interest in Sonya.

During his last days home before returning to the front, Nicholas feels the typical atmosphere of love within the Rostov family disturbed by tensions between his cousin Sonya and his friend Dolokhov. Nicholas discovers that Dolokhov has asked for Sonya's hand in marriage, but Sonya has refused him, clinging to her love for Nicholas. Nicholas begs Sonya to reconsider Dolokhov's offer, but she insists that she loves Nicholas like a brother, and that such love is enough for her.

Meanwhile, Denisov develops an interest in Natasha, with whom he dances splendidly at a ball. Dolokhov invites Nicholas to a card game at his hotel, and Nicholas loses all the money his father has given him and more—the final sum Nicholas owes Dolokhov is forty-three thousand rubles. Nicholas despairs, promising to pay the sum the next day, and he returns home in a gloomy mood. Hearing Natasha sing, however, makes Nicholas forget his woes momentarily. He asks his father for the money to pay Dolokhov, but it takes the old Count two weeks to raise the requested amount. Denisov proposes to Natasha, but is rejected. Both Denisov and Nicholas leave Moscow in disappointment.

## BOOK FIVE, CHAPTERS 1–5

> *Pierre began to feel a sense of uneasiness, and the need,*
> *even the inevitability, of entering into conversation with*
> *this stranger.* (See QUOTATIONS, p. 71)

Pierre is at the Torzhok railway station, en route to St. Petersburg after leaving his wife. He is miserable and lost, meditating on the absurdity of human life. Pierre watches a strange, old traveler wearing a Masonic ring. The man fascinates Pierre and unsettles him by gazing steadily at him. The stranger knows Pierre and addresses him, and the two launch into a deep philosophical conversation about human failings, divine perfection, and the possibility of reforming one's life. Pierre recognizes how awful his behavior has been, and he asks for guidance. The traveler—who Pierre later finds out is a Freemason named Bazdeev—tells Pierre to contact a Count Willarski in St. Petersburg.

After arriving in St. Petersburg, Pierre continues his spiritual search. Willarski visits him and proposes to sponsor him as an initiate into the Masonic brotherhood. At the initiation ritual, Pierre renounces his atheism, affirms his faith in God, and vows to love death as a deliverance from the woes of life. He gives up his valuables and confesses that his chief sin has been his passion for women. After this confession, Pierre feels bliss.

The following day, Vasili Kuragin visits Pierre and urges him to reconcile with Helene. In a new show of boldness, Pierre asks Vasili to leave, renouncing his earlier mistakes. Pierre then sets out for his southern estates. Meanwhile, Anna Pavlovna continues to give her customary parties, and takes a new interest in Boris, who has found great recent success as a military officer and diplomatic assistant.

Anna Pavlovna introduces Boris to Helene, who asks him to come visit her. During his stay, Boris becomes a regular guest at Helene's.

## BOOK FIVE, CHAPTERS 6–18

As the war recommences late in 1806, old Prince Bolkonski is appointed a military commander despite his age. His son, Andrew, having renounced active warfare, takes a desk job under his father's command and stays home with his son and sister. While his baby son suffers from a high fever, Andrew receives a letter from his father with news of a Russian victory and orders to leave on a military errand. He refuses to leave until his son is better. Andrew reads letters from his friend Bilibin about the confusions and injustices of war, until he panics and fears his son is dead. As the baby's fever breaks, Andrew realizes that his son is the one good thing in his life.

At his vast estates near Kiev, Pierre attempts to reform his land management in accordance with his new Masonic moral principles. He orders his serfs to be freed, pregnant women to be exempt from work in the fields, and so on. His managers try to use Pierre's good-will to their own advantage, eventually persuading him that the peasants are better off in their current servitude. Seeing happy peasants on a visit to his lands, Pierre believes that he has done great good for them, unaware that most of his serfs endure even greater misery than before.

On his way back to St. Petersburg, Pierre visits Andrew, whom he finds much older and gloomier than he remembered. Andrew's philosophy of stoic indifference to the plight of serfs, and to the fight of good against evil, provokes strong resistance in the new Masonic convert Pierre. While Pierre secretly fears he cannot refute Andrew's grim philosophy, he tries to convince Andrew of the power of good in the universe beyond the fallen human world. Pierre's enthusiasm makes an impact, and Andrew begins to emerge out of his melancholy state.

Andrew and Pierre drive to Bald Hills and greet Andrew's sister, Mary, who is receiving some holy pilgrims. One pilgrim, Pelageya, tells a story of an icon that weeps holy oil. Andrew and Pierre gently ridicule the old woman, and Mary rebukes them. Old Prince Bolkonski returns home and welcomes Pierre, whom Mary and the whole household like.

Nicholas, back at the front with his hussar regiment, feels happy despite the hardships of wartime. The soldiers are starving and poorly clothed, but there is a feeling of camaraderie. Nicholas has

SUMMARY & ANALYSIS

resolved to repay his parents' forty-three thousand rubles. One day, Nicholas's friend Denisov seizes food from a provisions vehicle in order to feed his men. Forced to appear before the authorities to defend himself, Denisov finds that the officer who has been keeping food supplies from Denisov and Nicholas's regiment is Telyanin, the one whom Nicholas once accused of theft. Denisov reponds violently, and soon faces a court-martial. Before the court-martial can take place, however, Denisov is wounded, and he takes the opportunity to go to the hospital instead of the military tribunal.

During the break provided by an armistice, Nicholas goes to visit Denisov in a Prussian military hospital, where he is horrified to find four hundred wounded soldiers. The patients are all neglected and threatened by typhus, and the army doctor cannot remember who Denisov is or whether he is still alive. Nicholas is shocked. Finally he finds Tushin, whom he had met at the battle of Schoen Graben, as well as Denisov, who seems strangely indifferent to Nicholas's arrival. Nicholas tries to persuade Denisov to seek a pardon from the tsar, but Denisov initially refuses out of a sense of honor. Finally, Denisov signs a simple and unspecific request for a pardon. Nicholas leaves to deliver this letter to the tsar, who is meeting with Napoleon at Tilsit.

At Tilsit, Nicholas meets up with his old friend Boris, who socializes with important Russian and French personages during the Tilsit meeting. Boris seems annoyed by Nicholas's arrival, but offers advice, recommending that Nicholas give Denisov's letter to an army commander rather than to the stern tsar. Aware that Boris is unwilling to help him, Nicholas decides that his only chance to help Denisov is through direct appeal to the tsar, whom he goes to visit despite being illegally dressed in civilian clothes. A general hears Nicholas's story and speaks to the tsar, but the tsar says he can do nothing, as the law is stronger than he is.

At a meeting between Napoleon and the tsar, Napoleon offers to give the Legion of Honor to the bravest of the Russian soldiers. An aide to the tsar chooses a soldier named Lazarev, almost at random. Nicholas is dismayed by the falsity of this award, especially in light of Denisov's unfair plight.

## ANALYSIS: BOOKS FOUR–FIVE

Just as Books Two and Three explore disillusionment with ideals of war and leadership, Book Four explores disillusionment with marriage. In the previous section, Andrew enters battle with a lofty ideal of glory and greatness; here, Pierre enters marriage with some optimism about his future life with Helene. Just as Andrew's idealistic notions are quickly debunked, Pierre's illusions of marital sanctity and respect fade when it appears that Helene has been unfaithful, and is only too happy to separate from him—provided he share his wealth. Pierre's disillusionment, like Andrew's, haunts him for many years.

The depressed Pierre initially searches for solace in religion, recalling Tolstoy's own intense religious fundamentalism later in life. Indeed, this religious or spiritual exploration, an important element of *War and Peace,* is perhaps most notable in Pierre's sudden conversion to Freemasonry through his encounter with the mysterious stranger in the Torzhok station. Tolstoy's portrait of the old Mason is otherworldly and even spooky, a great contrast to the author's normally highly realistic portrayals of his characters. The stranger, with his curious ring and his servant who seems never to need to shave, stands out as an almost supernatural element. Pierre's initiation ritual, in which he is undressed and blindfolded, is an equally surreal addition to the novel's realistic tone. The strangeness of these passages reinforces exactly what the alienated Pierre is seeking—an alternative to the reality of his despised everyday life, a leap into a different and better world. In a life full of confusions and minor immoralities, the appeal of the Masons' faith in a simple struggle between good and evil is powerful to Pierre and also to Andrew, who feels swayed by his friend's discussion of Freemasonry despite his initial skepticism.

Tolstoy's religious exploration also finds expression in Princess Mary's profound Christian devotion to her father. Mary cares for her father to the extent of sacrificing her own wishes for his well being, as she has renounced hopes of marriage. Living at Bald Hills, solving geometry problems far from society, Mary is like a nun in a cloister. Whenever her father is harsh and irritable toward her, she turns the other cheek meekly. As we have seen in Book One, Mary's letters to Julie recommend spirituality as the only defense against the cruel whims of fate. Here, we see that Mary's favorite entertainment is receiving the holy pilgrims who wander the countryside in chains, seeking mortification of the flesh in order to better understand God. Mary is so moved by the pilgrims that she even feels guilty at her love for her family, a love that she fears should be more rightly directed toward heaven.

The pervasive disillusionment that we have seen thus far in *War and Peace* suggests, though, that both Pierre's and Mary's religious feelings may ultimately prove to be misdirected. Indeed, as we see soon in Book Five, Pierre's well-meaning efforts to liberate and educate his serfs actually leave the serfs worse off, and leave Pierre self-deceived. Later, Pierre realizes the limitations of Freemasonry, growing impatient with its mysticism and passivity. His discontentment turns to open rebellion when he delivers a speech at the Masonic lodge, after which his religious faith fizzles away almost completely. Mary's faith does not disappear, but it seems equally misdirected: her father's mistreatment grows increasingly tyrannical, and Mary's nun-like isolation from the world makes her more and more irritable, even affecting her relations with her beloved nephew. As with Pierre's Freemasonry, Mary's Christianity begins to seem less like a source of strength in life, and more like a liability. Tolstoy does not critique the whole idea of faith, but only shows the limitations of two particular versions of it, inviting us to anticipate better alternatives that appear later in the novel.

## BOOKS SIX–SEVEN

### BOOK SIX, CHAPTERS 1–7

By 1809, France and Russia have become temporary allies—even against Austria, Russia's former ally. Daily life in Russia continues as usual. Andrew has been leading a secluded life for two years, busy at his estate with reading, writing analyses of recent military campaigns, and farm management. His practical intelligence has served him well as a landowner, and he has carried out the noble plans that Pierre aimed for but could not effect on his own estates. Andrew has freed all his serfs and made them wage-earners, one of the first examples of this social advancement in all of Russia. However, he still feels that his heart is old and dead.

On a household errand, Andrew dwells on his joyless mood, focusing on a dead oak as a symbol of his emotional state. Later, he visits the old Count Rostov on business at the latter's estate, Otradnoe. Andrew sees Natasha running in the fields and is struck by her cheerfulness. Annoyed because he is forced to stay at Otradnoe, he hears girls' voices singing on a balcony late one night, and his heart is troubled by youthful emotions. He sees the oak again, now in bloom. Andrew decides to go to St. Petersburg, not fully understanding the new life blossoming within him.

Arriving in the capital, Andrew meets Tsar Alexander; his secretary of state, Speranski; and his minister of war, Arakcheev. The men are engaged in liberal reforms of the state. Andrew, who has drawn up a more liberal set of military laws, has submitted them to the tsar for consideration. Arakcheev criticizes Andrew's proposal, but makes him a member of the military reform committee. Andrew, courted as a great liberal, also meets Speranski, though the two men disagree on the question of special privileges to noblemen. Andrew feels that honor is a positive principle by which to guide behavior, while Speranski believes it to be a spur to superficial rewards. Nevertheless, Speranski agrees to meet with Andrew again. Andrew feels awe at Speranski's vast intellect and cool logic, and he treats the man as an equal. Andrew receives an invitation to join the committee in charge of drawing up a new civil code.

In St. Petersburg, Pierre continues his charitable work on behalf of the Masonic brotherhood, but he grows impatient of the brotherhood's passivity and dissatisfied with its mysticism. Pierre goes to western Europe to seek illumination from other Masons and returns to St. Petersburg counseling action. Many of his fellow Masons accuse him of revolutionary sympathies, and Pierre becomes disgruntled. His estranged wife, Helene, returns from abroad and seeks reconciliation with him, as does his wife's family. In a forgiving mood, Pierre returns to Helene and they live together once again. Helene had enjoyed great success during the meetings between the French and the Russians, and has achieved an international reputation for being intelligent as well as beautiful—a judgment that perplexes Pierre. Pierre, while playing his role as the crank husband of a distinguished wife, privately continues his spiritual self-investigation, recording in his diary his struggle with a jealous hatred of Boris. Pierre recounts his dreams of his spiritual master, Joseph Alexeevich, and seeks fortitude to withstand the temptations of debauchery and sloth.

Count Rostov, suffering from financial worries, decides to take his family to St. Petersburg and seek employment there. The Rostovs, however, are outsiders in St. Petersburg, and have trouble fitting in to the local society. As no one proposes marriage to Vera Rostova, she accepts an offer from Berg, who is candid about his need for Vera's dowry to help set up a household with her. Count Rostov is embarrassed to say that he has little financial means to provide Vera with a dowry, but in the end he promises Berg twenty thousand rubles in cash, along with a promise of eighty thousand more later.

Meanwhile, Natasha, now sixteen, thinks often of Boris, wondering whether or not his earlier offer of marriage was a joke. Boris comes to visit the Rostovs in St. Petersburg and is struck by Natasha's beauty. Although aware that marriage to a girl without a dowry would bring him failure, he cannot help visiting the Rostovs every day, despite Helene's anger. Natasha, for her part, seems equally smitten with Boris.

### BOOK SIX, CHAPTERS 8–17

The Countess Rostova tells Natasha that, despite the mutual affection Natasha and Boris share, there is no hope of her marrying Boris, as he is poor and a relation. The countess also feels Natasha does not truly love Boris. Natasha is not too distraught at the news. The countess informs Boris of her decision, and Boris no longer frequents the Rostovs' home. On New Year's Eve, a grand ball is held, which the tsar attends and to which the Rostovs are invited. It is Natasha's first society ball, and she and the other women attend to their toilettes with care. Accompanied by the Rostovs' friend Peronskaya, the young women enter the ballroom, the splendor of which dazzles Natasha. She sees Andrew, Pierre, Helene, Anatole, and others. The tsar makes his appearance, and the music and dancing begin.

Natasha is worried that no one will ask her to dance, but at Pierre's instigation, Andrew takes her to the dance floor, where her innocent young beauty contrasts with Helene's hardened attractiveness. Many men then ask Natasha to dance, and she is overjoyed. Andrew finds himself toying with the idea of marrying her. Natasha greets Pierre, who is gloomy and wonders why he does not enjoy himself more. Andrew goes to a party at Speranski's home, but is bored by the guests' superficial laughter. Andrew goes home distressed by the useless labor he has performed working for the cause of social reform in Russia. The next day, he visits the Rostov home, stays for dinner, and hears Natasha sing. Impressed by Natasha as ever, he resolves to start living more deeply.

Berg and Vera, installed in their new residence, host a party to which Pierre, the Rostovs, and Boris are invited. Berg and Vera are delighted to see that they have imitated the style of similar parties exactly. Pierre notices that Natasha appears less radiantly beautiful than usual, until Andrew addresses a few words to her and her spirit lights up. Pierre wonders what is developing between Andrew and Natasha, with confusion in his own heart. Andrew asks about Boris's childhood promise to marry Natasha. The next day, Andrew dines at the Rostovs' home, and everyone knows he is there for Natasha's sake. Marriage seems a possibility. Natasha confesses to her mother her love for Andrew, while Andrew confesses to Pierre his love for Natasha. Pierre counsels Andrew to marry her, though he feels gloomy at the thought of Andrew's happiness. Andrew tells his father of his plan to marry Natasha, and the old man advises taking time to think it over. Andrew stays away from St. Petersburg for a time, causing Natasha great anxiety. Ultimately, however, Natasha controls her feelings and tells herself she is self-contented, needing no one else to be happy.

Andrew reappears at the Rostovs, informing them of his desire to marry their daughter. They agree. Andrew asks Natasha for her hand, telling her that unfortunately they must wait a year. Natasha is distraught at the delay, but tearfully accepts his offer. Andrew refuses to limit Natasha's freedom by announcing their engagement, telling her that she may call it off at any moment in the coming year. He tells her he must go away for a long time. She suffers for two weeks after his departure, then recovers.

At Bald Hills, the old Prince Bolkonski becomes grumpy after Andrew's departure. He treats his daughter Mary with extreme harshness, though she finds it easy to forgive him. She counsels religion in letters to her friend Julie Karagina in St. Petersburg, who is mourning her brother killed in action. Mary says that faith is the only consolation to the ravages of destiny, which can kill off an angel like Lise. She reports that Andrew has become more sickly and nervous since his return from St. Petersburg, and that he shares her belief that he will not marry Natasha. Mary thinks that Andrew is too devoted to his first wife to ever accept a replacement. The old prince continues to take out his anger at his son's wish to marry Natasha by treating Mary badly, and by threatening to marry Mademoiselle Bourienne. Mary takes solace in the pilgrims who visit her in secret, especially an old woman named Theodosia who goes around in chains. Mary wishes to emulate Theodosia, and is ashamed that she loves her family more than God.

## BOOK SEVEN

On the front, Nicholas enjoys an idle military life with his comrades until he receives troubling letters from home about the Rostovs' financial problems. One especially imploring letter from his mother persuades Nicholas to seek leave and return to Otradnoe, the family estate. He congratulates his sister Natasha on her engagement to Andrew, but privately wonders why Andrew is staying away for so long, concluding that his health must be the reason.

Visiting his father's manager, Mitenka, in an attempt to put his family's finances in order, Nicholas explodes in anger, convinced that Mitenka has been embezzling. Nicholas's father urges him to calm down, and Nicholas agrees not to get involved in financial matters again, turning his attention to the hunt instead. One bright fall day, Nicholas and his huntsman, Daniel, are preparing to depart when Natasha appears, expressing her resolve to go along. Despite Daniel's dismay, Natasha joins the hunting party, which sets out with over a hundred dogs. She proves she can ride beautifully, while the count earns the censure of one of his serfs for letting a wolf get away.

At his hunting post, Nicholas hopes to earn the prestige of downing a wolf. Finally he sees a wolf ambling along and calls for his hounds to pursue it. Nicholas's favorite dog, Karay, nearly kills the wolf, but it shakes itself free and continues on. Other huntsmen's dogs catch it. Bound, the wolf glares wildly at its captors. Later, the huntsmen pursue a fox until a hound from another hunting party catches it. Nicholas is irate, knowing the hound belongs to their neighbor, Ilagin. To apologize, Ilagin invites the Rostovs to hunt hares on his own property. They do so, and they catch a hare. The party spends the night in a peasant village, where they are regaled with home-cooked food and balalaika music. The peasant huntsman sings so beautifully that Natasha decides to learn to play the guitar. As Nicholas and Natasha ride home in a buggy, she declares that she will never be so happy again.

The Rostovs' financial problems become so acute that they consider selling their family home, Otradnoe. The only solution seems to be in marrying Nicholas off to a rich heiress like Julie Karagina, whom the countess selects carefully. Julie's parents are willing, but Nicholas is unwilling, invoking his honor and arguing that love should be more important than money. Meanwhile, Andrew writes to Natasha, saying that his health has forced him to stay abroad a bit longer. Natasha is bored and restless waiting for Andrew. She,

Sonya, and Nicholas philosophize about happiness, reminisce about childhood, and put on costumes to entertain the Rostov household.

Sonya, Natasha, and Nicholas drive out to neighbors to entertain them also. Nicholas is conscious of loving Sonya, disguised now as a man. At the neighbor's home, he dares to take her in his arms and kiss her. Natasha congratulates Nicholas. Back at home, the girls gaze in mirrors to see their fortunes. Sonya pretends to see Andrew lying down and looking happy, and then something blue and red, evoking the way Natasha once described Pierre as a blue and red object. Nicholas's parents criticize his decision to marry Sonya, saying that he is free to marry whom he wishes, but that they will never treat the gold-digger Sonya as a daughter. Nicholas is saddened, but he remains firm in his resolve to marry Sonya. He returns to the front.

---

## ANALYSIS: BOOKS SIX–SEVEN

The character of Natasha emerges gloriously in these chapters, and acquires deep symbolic significance. Natasha is more than a mere girl, though neither especially beautiful nor clever, and less morally serious than women like Princess Mary. Natasha's great power lies not in specific attributes, but in her extraordinary vitality. When she runs in a yellow dress alongside Andrew's carriage, or sings on the balcony, or swoons over a simple Russian folk song, she is doing no more than living. Yet she is alive with a force and an enthusiasm that no other character in the novel possesses. It is almost a mystical power, which explains why none of the men infatuated with her—including Andrew and Pierre—seem able to recognize that Natasha is the cause of the spiritual changes within themselves after they spend time with her. Andrew hears Natasha sing, but then falls asleep unsure of where the youthful confusions in his heart come from. Pierre is dejected after learning of Natasha's engagement to Andrew, but fails to recognize his dejection as disappointment. Natasha works below the consciousness of these men, like a vital force beyond rational understanding.

The Rostovs' financial problems are an important element in the novel, as they direct our attention to the changing social and economic climate in Russia. The Rostovs' simple and old-fashioned charms—their hospitality, their love of the hunt, their largesse with gifts—are a liability in the modern world. Their grace and friendliness contrast sharply with the cool and calculating ways of Vasili Kuragin and his hardhearted children. Yet, sadly, the Kuragins' fortunes are growing at an astonishing pace, as the children make brilliant matches with wealthy spouses due largely to their father's maneuverings. By contrast, Berg very nearly rejects Vera Rostov as a consequence of Count Rostov's mismanagement of money affairs. The decline in the Rostov fortunes is not due to overly luxurious living but to simple obliviousness. Nicholas's loss at cards illustrates this obliviousness, as he squanders money not because of a weakness for women or horses, but because he does not understand that his opponent at cards is angry and jealous that Sonya prefers Nicholas. It is this naïve good faith and carefree lifestyle that is costing the Rostovs their wealth and standing.

The multiple marriages in *War and Peace* remind us of the variety of motives for choosing a particular mate. Spouses may be selected for reasons that are sentimental or practical, self-serving or altruistic, self-deceiving or wise; Tolstoy, who suffered in his own marriage, is aware of all of these possibilities. Pierre's disastrous decision to marry Helene is only an extreme form of the blindness that frequently overtakes various individuals in the courtship rituals we see in the novel. In Book Eight, Julie Karagina's foolish denial of Boris's fortune hunting shows us how close Mary might have come to a similar fate with the same suitor, as Mary feels just as desperate for marriage as Julie. Andrew's suitability as a husband for Natasha is in doubt, despite the evidence of love and affection on both sides. These doubts arise partly because we know that Andrew was dissatisfied even with his angelic first wife, Lise, whom all have described as a paragon of virtuous womanhood. The only real hope for marriage at this point in the novel is in Nicholas's proposal to Sonya, which has arisen not out of a desire for money, but out of sincere feeling.

## BOOKS EIGHT–NINE

### BOOK EIGHT, CHAPTERS 1–7
Upon the news of Natasha and Andrew's engagement and the death of his Masonic benefactor Bazdeev, Pierre loses interest in his life and becomes depressed, abandoning his Masonic activities. He moves to Moscow, but does little besides read and party. He feels disappointed in himself and in the world of falsity around him.

Meanwhile, old Prince Bolkonski also moves his household to Moscow. The anti-French sentiment prevalent in the city puts him in the center of the opposition to the government. He is more crotchety than ever, and is growing senile and forgetful. Mary regrets the move. She feels isolated, is alienated by her friend Julie's whirlwind social life, and misses the visits from the religious pilgrims. Mary becomes irritable in her lessons with her little nephew. Despite her promise to Andrew to prepare their father for Andrew's marriage to Natasha, Mary is afraid to bring up the subject.

The old Prince Bolkonski continues to show great affection toward Mademoiselle Bourienne, whom he may seriously consider marrying. He churlishly kicks out of his house a renowned French doctor who has been sent to care for him, accusing the man of being a spy. The prince continues to socialize with old acquaintants, imposing his spy stories and his anti-French ideas upon them.

Pierre warns Mary that Boris is paying court to her in hopes of winning her heiress's fortune in marriage—just as he is with Julie. Mary confides to Pierre her wish to marry *anyone* in order to escape her overcritical father. Boris, while preferring Mary to Julie, is pushed to propose to the artificial and aging Julie, due to a threat that Anatole Kuragin will propose if Boris does not. Julie delightedly accepts Boris's proposal, and the wedding plans are announced.

Count Rostov, accompanied by Sonya and Natasha, goes to Moscow to complete the sale of Otradnoe, to order Natasha's wedding trousseau, and to present Natasha to Andrew, who is expected soon. As their home is unheated, the Rostovs stay with their old friend Marya Dmitrievna, who helps Natasha select wedding clothes and gives her advice on how to handle her future father-in-law. The next day, Count Rostov takes Natasha to visit the old Prince Bolkonski. Despite her self-confidence, Natasha is wary. Princess Mary takes an instant dislike to Natasha, whom she views as frivolous, and the prince grumpily refuses to meet with the Rostovs. Natasha, for her part, finds Mary dry and boring. After a long silence, Mary forces herself to wish Natasha well, but both women feel the falseness of the words. Natasha leaves, and cries about the meeting.

## Book Eight, Chapters 8–22

At the opera that evening, Natasha muses that everything would be fine if only Andrew returned. She sees Boris, Julie, and Helene, and is conscious that all of them are staring at her. Natasha turns her attention to the opera, but Anatole Kuragin addresses her, eyeing her shoulders with interest. Natasha is agitated, and tries to watch the opera but sees only absurd falsity in it.

The spendthrift Anatole has been sent to Moscow in the hopes that he will moderate his expenditures and find an heiress wife. He lives a thoughtless and selfish life, hiding the fact that he is secretly married, and goes around in the company of Dolokhov. Anatole is attracted to Natasha, and Natasha is vaguely interested in Anatole as well, though she still waits for Andrew's return. Helene visits Natasha, pays compliments that make Natasha love her, and invites Natasha to a gathering at which Anatole will be present. At Helene's party, full of disreputable people, Anatole dances with Natasha and tells her he loves her madly. That night, Natasha is tormented by doubt as to whether she loves Andrew or Anatole, feeling she loves them both.

The Rostovs' hostess, Marya Dmitrievna, decides it best for the Rostovs to return to Otradnoe in order to avoid fighting with the irritable old Prince Bolkonski. Natasha is upset, especially when she receives a letter from Mary begging forgiveness for her rudeness, and another from Anatole declaring love. Natasha decides she loves Anatole. While Natasha sleeps, Sonya reads Anatole's love letter to Natasha, questions her, and threatens to reveal the secret love. Natasha becomes angry with Sonya and affirms her feelings for Anatole, resolving to break off the engagement with Andrew and elope with Anatole. Anatole and Dolokhov obtain money and horses for the elopement. But at the moment of departure, a footman arrives and orders Anatole to be brought to Marya Dmitrievna to forestall the elopement. Anatole barely escapes. Marya Dmitrievna is furious with Natasha for carrying on with Anatole in her own house, but she promises not to tell Count Rostov about the elopement plans. Pierre is summoned to Marya Dmitrievna's house and is told of Anatole's plans.

Pierre informs everyone at the house that Anatole is already married to a girl in Poland. The enraged Pierre hunts down Anatole and orders him out of Moscow immediately. Anatole is indignant, but leaves the next day. Natasha falls ill, and is discovered to have attempted to poison herself. Pierre visits Andrew, who is back in Moscow. Andrew's connections with Speranski are finished, as Speranski has recently fallen from grace, accused of treachery and forced into exile.

Andrew returns Natasha's portrait, absolutely refusing to forgive her for entertaining thoughts of elopement with Anatole. Andrew assigns Pierre the task of telling Natasha that Andrew has rejected her. Pierre visits Natasha, but she already knows the news he is delivering. She is full of self-blame. Pierre is tender toward Natasha. He watches the comet of 1812 with a sense of a new life blossoming.

BOOK NINE, CHAPTERS 1–12

On June 12, 1812, the French forces cross Russia's frontiers. The narrator explores the question of what caused this invasion, disagreeing with the historians' answers to this problem. The invasion, the narrator argues, comes about not because of diplomatic errors or strategic decisions alone, but because of a coincidence of millions of small causal events. Even the great leaders Napoleon and Alexander are not responsible for the events of 1812. Like all men, they imagine themselves acting independently, but are really the slaves of circumstance. There is, therefore, no rational explanation for history.

In Prussia, Napoleon prepares to head eastward, and the sight of him inspires Polish officers to a suicidal plunge into the river, hoping to impress him. Forty officers die during this feat. Meanwhile, on the Russian side, confusion reigns at Vilna, and no defense strategy has yet been chosen. The tsar attends a ball his aides have thrown, at which Helene and Boris, now rich and powerful, are present.

The tsar writes Napoleon a polite note asking whether Napoleon's crossing of the Niemen River is indeed intended as an act of invasion. The tsar sends General Balashev on a diplomatic mission to deliver the note. On his way, Balashev meets the French commander Murat, and during their discussion, each side claims that the other is the aggressor in the war. Upon reaching Napoleon's camp, Balashev is surprised at the rude treatment he receives from the French soldiers and Napoleon's chief of war, Davout. Napoleon summons Balashev for a meeting at which Napoleon talks incessantly, irrationally attempting to justify France's invasion and trying to impress Balashev with the French army's superiority. Napoleon is utterly convinced by the lies he utters. Later, Napoleon invites Balashev to dinner and is cordial toward him.

Andrew goes to St. Petersburg, receives an appointment on Kutuzov's staff, and unsuccessfully attempts to challenge Anatole Kuragin to a duel for his plans to elope with Natasha. After some military service in Turkey, Andrew asks General Kutuzov for a transfer to the western front. On the way, Andrew stops at Bald Hills, where he finds everyone unchanged except for his young son, who is quickly growing up. Still aware of Prince Bolkonski's mistreatment of Mary, Andrew speaks to his father and blames Mademoiselle Bourienne for stirring up discord between father and daughter. The old prince tells Andrew to leave, and Andrew does so without reconciling with his father. Mary urges Andrew to forgive their father, saying that men are never to blame and that evils come from heaven.

On the western front, Andrew encounters massive confusion, with hard-nosed strategists opposing proponents of bold action, and both groups opposing the majority that simply wants a situation beneficial to them. Andrew is summoned to meet with the tsar and his military advisors, who disagree in a hodgepodge of European languages. When Andrew's opinion is requested, he responds that he does not know enough to offer one, which angers the advisors. When the tsar asks Andrew where he would like to serve, Andrew irrevocably loses favor by stating his preference to serve in the army instead of remaining with the tsar.

The Rostovs write letters to Nicholas on the front, imploring him to come home. He replies to these letters, and separately to Sonya as well, that honor must keep him serving in the army in wartime. Nicholas's regiment moves into Poland with great excitement. A devoted young officer named Ilyin serves Nicholas, and invites him one rainy day to take shelter in a nearby tavern. At the tavern, Ilyin tempts Nicholas by telling him that a certain Mary Hendrikhovna—on whom Nicholas has a crush—is present.

### Book Nine, Chapters 13–23

In the tavern, all the officers are in love with Mary Hendrikhovna, the beautiful wife of an army doctor. The men jokingly flirt with her even in the presence of her beleaguered husband. Early in the morning, on his way back to the regiment from the tavern, Nicholas is roused by the sound of gunfire. He knows that the battle has begun. Seeing an opportunity for attack, Nicholas speaks to his commander, but rushes into a charge on the French before an order has been given. He cuts the arm of a French soldier, who instantly surrenders in fear. Nicholas is recommended for military honors, but inwardly he is disappointed that his alleged heroism means only that someone else is more scared than he is.

In Moscow, the Rostovs are troubled by the fact that Natasha has been ill. Expensive doctors are called, and they have diverging medical opinions. Though family and patient alike are relieved by the show of medical attention, the real cause of Natasha's malady is her hurt feelings, not any physical ailment. Gradually she begins to improve, though she is not happy and feels no urge to sing or laugh as before. Natasha takes solace only in Pierre's visits and caring company, and in a new religious devotion she has developed under the influence of Agrafena, a visiting neighbor. As news of Russia's dire military situation spreads through Moscow, with rumors that only a miracle can save the nation, the Rostovs go to church. Natasha is aware that people are talking about her. She prays and feels the joyful possibility of a new and better life for herself. The liturgy affects Natasha greatly, and she feels that God has heard her prayer.

Pierre, meanwhile, is deeply pleased by his visits to Natasha, feeling a new vitality within himself. Applying a secret code the Masons revealed to him, he prophetically predicts that Napoleon is the Antichrist and will be defeated by the tsar in 1812, under Pierre's leadership. Pierre, visiting the Rostovs to inform them that Nicholas has received military honors, finds Natasha much improved in spirits. The tsar makes an appeal to Muscovites, asking for sacrifices to save the country. Sonya reads the tsar's appeal out loud to the Rostovs. The count declares that no sacrifice is too great. Natasha's younger brother, Petya, declares his wish to enter the army. When his father resists, Petya cries. Meanwhile, the developing love between Natasha and Pierre is becoming increasingly clear to both of them. The next morning, Petya sets off for the Kremlin to join the hussars. Amid the crushing crowds, Petya is overjoyed to glimpse the tsar and becomes even more determined to join the army.

Pierre attends a conference of noblemen that has gathered to reply to the tsar's appeal for aid. Against loud avowals of patriotism, Pierre speaks out in favor of practical strategy. The crowd is irrational, approving oversimplified versions of the Russian crisis and ignoring Pierre's voice of reason. The tsar enters the hall and addresses the noblemen, sincerely thanking them for their loyalty. The noblemen and merchants weep in devotion to their leader, offering him everything they have. Count Rostov goes off to enroll Petya in the army, abandoning his earlier opposition. Even Pierre, swept away by patriotic emotion, feels ashamed of his earlier rational comments.

## ANALYSIS: BOOKS EIGHT–NINE

Natasha's romantic woes in these sections bring about a great deal of change in her character. Up to this point, she has always been a child of nature, carefree and happy, falling in love with man after man with childlike innocence. With Andrew's departure for Europe, however, Natasha is forced to see love not as a carefree joy, but as a test. As time passes, she becomes less able to assure herself that a year of waiting will make no difference to her commitment to Andrew—and her infatuation with Anatole Kuragin destroys that commitment entirely. In Anatole's so-called love for Natasha, Tolstoy shows us that love may not be an obvious emotional state, but may also be an illusion. We also see this illusory nature of love in Nicholas's crush on Mary Hendrikhovna. Though Nicholas appears to have real affection for Mary Hendrikhovna, we see that all the officers have crushes on her, simply because they are starved for female companionship—not because of any real or lasting love. In this manner, Tolstoy establishes love as yet another ideal, like patriotism or religious faith, that comes into question as *War and Peace* unfolds.

Tolstoy also uses these chapters to explore the unpredictable irrationality of historical events, which becomes a symbol of the absurdity of human existence. The narrator makes an unusual direct aside to us, explaining that it is not great men who make history, but rather a vast network of tiny chains of cause and effect that no one, even emperors, can control. We see that neither Napoleon nor Tsar Alexander is in full control of the military situation. Both leaders, swept along by events as they unfold, are merely doing their best to pretend to be in control. The tsar's military advisors can agree on nothing, and the Russian and French commanders disagree about which side is the aggressor in the war. Moreover, Tolstoy implies that what is true in war is true in all human endeavors. Even the best laid plans end up having no importance, as Andrew learns when all his work in developing a new civil code is rendered worthless for purely random reasons. Speranski's sudden and unexplainable fall from grace, due to vague allegations of treachery, similarly invalidates all of Speranski's work. In an unpredictable world, the most successful may be those who follow their instincts of the moment, like Nicholas when he rushes into battle without waiting for orders.

The intriguing character of Napoleon offers us a surprising, up-close portrait of the leader as an egomaniac. Contrary to our expectations, Napoleon is not gifted with superior rational powers. His stream of chitchat with the Russian General Balashev, steamrollering over his conversation partner in a way that leaves no room for contradiction or questioning, is based almost exclusively on outright lies. Napoleon claims the Poles as his allies, for instance, all the while knowing this assertion to be untrue. Napoleon's genius lies not in his powers of reason, but in his conviction that he is absolutely right in all matters. He ends his conference with Balashev by mentally communicating to the latter "I have convinced you"—indicating the irrational self-confidence that seems to be the primary secret behind his stellar success at world domination. More broadly, Tolstoy uses Napoleon's brand of authoritative falsehood to bring to the forefront the broader issue of the subjectivity of reality. If Napoleon is so effectively able to impose his views of reality upon others, we wonder who else in the novel is doing the same.

# BOOK TEN

### BOOK TEN, CHAPTERS 1–12

The narrator tells us that the historical accounts of Napoleon's 1812 invasion of Russia are oversimplified and false. Napoleon did not rationally calculate the risk of invading Russia, but went in unaware of the dangers of a Russian winter. By the same token, Tsar Alexander did not lure the French into the Russian heartland, but on the contrary wished to keep them out. History has been written after the fact to lend a rational and intentional character to what originally were almost random events.

At Bald Hills, Mary endures her father's blame for his quarrel with Andrew. She has only a vague understanding of the wars, and fears for her brother's life. Her father still insists that Russia is safe, ignoring news that the French have already crossed Russian borders, and dismissing Andrew's letter warning that their position at Bald Hills is dangerous. Increasingly grouchy and senile, the old prince occupies himself with his garden, construction on his estate, and his will and testament. Meanwhile, the prince's servant Alpatych goes to the city of Smolensk to ask the governor about the risks of staying at Bald Hills. Gunfire is heard near Smolensk, indicating that the French are very close. The governor's official report claims that Smolensk is safe, but, off the record, the governor recommends that the Bolkonskis go to Moscow. On the streets, people flee in terror, and the townspeople set Smolensk on fire to thwart the invaders.

By chance, Alpatych encounters Andrew, who writes a letter to Bald Hills telling his father and sister that it is urgent they flee to Moscow immediately. Andrew leads his regiment in retreat in the midst of a drought, his worldview altered by the abandonment and burning of Smolensk. He visits Bald Hills, now abandoned. The ruined fields and empty house deeply move him, and the sight of his soldiers bathing naked in a dirty pond—as cannon fodder—depresses and disgusts him.

In St. Petersburg, Helene's and Anna Pavlovna's salons continue almost unaffected by Napoleon's invasion, with each salon holding a different opinion of the war. When Kutuzov is made commander in chief to heighten Russian military unity, he earns great praise, whereas earlier he had been criticized.

Napoleon, meanwhile, prepares to march upon Moscow. The narrator writes that historians overestimate the rationality behind Napoleon's decision to march and his cunning use of a Cossack informer, Lavrushka, who, in reality, was a drunken looter.

The old prince and Mary are not in Moscow, but rather at Andrew's estate at Bogucharovo, where the prince has been taken after a paralytic attack. He is too ill to travel, but Mary fears for his safety as the French approach. Tearfully, the prince finally expresses gratitude to his daughter for her lifetime of devotion to him. A local official arrives to tell Mary that she must leave, and she returns to the bedroom to find her father has died. Meanwhile, Bagration writes to the Minister of War to present the debacle in Smolensk in the best possible light. Alpatych tries unsuccessfully to force the local Bogucharovo peasants to relocate to Moscow.

After her father's funeral, Mary lies in her bedroom until Mademoiselle Bourienne suggests that they ask the invading French forces for protection. But there are no horses to take her away, and the peasants are starving. Mary offers the peasants the grain stored at Bogucharovo and urges them to leave with her. They refuse her offer, however, thinking she wants to trick them back into serfdom.

### BOOK TEN, CHAPTERS 13–24

Nicholas and two comrades ride to Bogucharovo by chance, not knowing it is a Bolkonski residence. Nicholas finds Mary stranded there, as the peasants refused to let her leave. He quickly brings order to the rioting peasants. On her way to Moscow, Mary thinks of Nicholas as her savior and wonders if she loves him. Nicholas too thinks of marrying her, a wealthy heiress and attractive as well.

Andrew, summoned to serve General Kutuzov, meets Denisov, now a lieutenant colonel, and reminisces privately about Natasha, whom Denisov had courted. Kutuzov arrives, fatter than ever. Andrew greets Kutuzov and tells him of Prince Bolkonski's death. Denisov presents to Kutuzov his plan for breaking the French lines of communication. Andrew observes Kutuzov's bored, faintly contemptuous seen-it-all attitude toward the officers reporting to him. At his lodging, Kutuzov interrupts his reading of a French novel to speak cordially with Andrew about the late old Prince Bolkonski and to voice frustration with military advisors. Andrew declines to serve the general at headquarters.

As the French approach Moscow, the behavior of the Muscovites becomes more frivolous. Violently anti-French publications are read throughout the city, and aristocrats try hard not to lapse into their habit of speaking French. Julie Drubetskaya, Boris's wife, prepares to flee. Pierre risks bankruptcy to finance his own regiment, but does not himself prepare to fight. Julie teases Pierre that he is defending Natasha's reputation for personal reasons, and also tells him that Mary is in town. Pierre is alarmed to realize that the French really will invade Moscow. Seeing a French cook being flogged as a spy, Pierre feels that he must leave the city. The thought of sacrificing his belongings for his country thrills him.

The Russian and French troops clash at the Battle of Borodino. The Russian forces are considerably weakened, though the narrator argues that Borodino can be viewed as a Russian spiritual victory. The narrator tells us that Russian historians have found a way to attribute the victory to Kutuzov's military genius, but these historians are wrong. According to the narrator, there is nothing strategic about the choice of Borodino as battle site; like everything else in history, Borodino is the product of happenstance.

Leaving Moscow, Pierre comes upon a convoy of wounded soldiers. An army doctor tells him they have less than a third of the wagons they need to cart away the wounded from the next day's battle. At Borodino, Pierre sees the French and the Russian encampments and watches a church procession in which Kutuzov kneels before a holy icon. Pierre encounters Boris Drubetskoy and also Dolokhov, who has weaseled his way into an important position. Dolokhov approaches Pierre and asks his forgiveness for past wrongs. Andrew, meanwhile, is miserable and disillusioned. He muses on his disillusionment with his ideals: he has lost faith in love and honor, in his father's trust in his homeland, and in Natasha's loyalty.

BOOK TEN, CHAPTERS 25–39

Pierre visits Andrew, who explains to him the folly of the military commanders and the unpredictability of war. Cynical about war in a general sense, Andrew still foresees a Russian victory at Borodino the next day. That night, he thinks of Natasha with longing.

In Napoleon's quarters, the French emperor is finishing his toilette and preparing for the battle on the Russian front. He receives a portrait of his son as a gift. He sends an inspirational proclamation to the troops, and then inspects the battle site, sending out meticulously detailed instructions as to the deployment of troops. The narrator says that none of these orders were ultimately followed during the battle. Mocking the theory that Napoleon did not win at Borodino because he had a cold, the narrator again muses that history is made by ordinary men following their own will.

The next morning, Pierre awakens to the sounds of battle. Enchanted by the beauty of the scene, he rides into the midst of the fighting to observe, unaware that he is at the heart of the battlefield. Pierre shows no fear, and the officers allow him to stay. When something explodes next to him, however, he becomes terrified. Pierre returns to the battery to find that the French have captured it and that his recent acquaintances have been killed.

Napoleon, meanwhile, is surveying the battle, but neither he nor his officers really understand what is happening. His officers request reinforcements, and he grows troubled. Finally, news that the French are not doing well reaches Napoleon. He sees the strange new effects of military failure on the faces of his troops. On the other side, Kutuzov decides against a retreat, and the message spreads throughout the Russian troops, inspiring them.

Andrew's regiment is still under heavy fire. He tries to encourage his troops, but he is wounded by an exploding shell and carried off in dazed confusion to the army hospital, conscious that there is something in life that he does not understand. In the military surgery unit, Andrew witnesses an amputation being performed next to him, and he recognizes the patient to be Anatole Kuragin. Andrew feels that compassion is the greatest human emotion.

Napoleon fails to feel any compunction when he muses on his defeat and all the lives lost. He rationalizes Borodino as merely an unfortunate miscalculation. Meanwhile, it rains on the field of corpses, and the soldiers are tired of killing. The narrator again muses on the irony that a bedraggled Russian army—one that lost a full half of its men—could be considered spiritually triumphant over the unstoppable French war machine. He concludes that the French were opposed by a spirit greater than their own.

---

### ANALYSIS: BOOK TEN

The fact that the French army invades as far as Bald Hills, the Bolkonski estate, is symbolic of the end of the old prince's seclusion from the modern world. A holdover from the bygone days of the previous tsar, resisting newfangled notions about modern statecraft and society, the old prince attempts to keep both himself and his daughter hidden away from the march of history. The eternal truths of geometry mean more to him than social progress or historical change. However, the prince's growing irritability during the war years shows that he is not at peace with himself. With Napoleon's entry into Smolensk, the prince's naïve faith in old-fashioned times comes to a painful end. In this regard, his death is a symbol of the end of the Russian old regime: Russia will never be the same after Napoleon. Tolstoy hints that the aristocracy will lose some of its old entitlements, as we see when Princess Mary is stranded at Bald Hills because her peasants refuse to harness her horses. Similarly, the nobleman Pierre, visiting the battlefield of Borodino as the bullets whiz past, appears absurdly out of place among the practical commoners who are accomplishing the bulk of the victory. We feel that the new Russia will be less aristocratic and more down to earth.

Tolstoy's final analysis of the Russian victory at Borodino amounts to a conclusion that a "greater spirit" than that of the French proves triumphant. The final conqueror of France has turned out to be neither brilliant Russian military strategy nor the unparalleled heroism of the Russian soldiers, but rather a mystical awareness of a Russian spiritual superiority. Tolstoy emphasizes that there is no rational explanation for why the French are not triumphant at Borodino. French troops significantly outnumber the Russians, yet somehow the ultimate spiritual victory is Russia's. Napoleon's self-serving rationalizations and shallow self-confidence have helped him conquer half of Europe, but they are no match for the grand spiritual example Kutuzov sets when he humbly kneels before a religious icon during a church procession. Napoleon believes in his own brilliance, but Kutuzov believes in something greater than himself. This belief is the same sense of belonging to the larger universe that Andrew contemplates when he stares at the sky at Austerlitz and that Pierre feels in his Masonic experiments. Tolstoy implies that, ultimately, it is humility rather than reason that emerges triumphant, whether on the battlefield or in the trials of everyday life.

# BOOK ELEVEN

### BOOK ELEVEN, CHAPTERS 1–9

With more comments on the infinite complexity of historical processes, the narrator tells us that Kutuzov warily reports a victory at Borodino but then decides to retreat beyond Moscow with his depleted army. Listening wearily to his disagreeing advisors, and despite the commander Bennigsen's firm refusal to abandon the Russian capital, Kutuzov realizes that Moscow must be left for the French. Privately, Kutuzov tries to understand how he ever allowed Napoleon to reach Moscow. Despite official orders not to flee, Muscovites leave the city, refusing to submit to French occupation.

Meanwhile, Helene has become romantically attached to a foreign prince and an old Russian grandee. She converts to Catholicism in the hopes of persuading the Pope to annul her marriage to Pierre, making a sizeable donation to the church at the same time. After some wavering, Helene settles on remarriage to the Russian grandee. She seeks divorce from Pierre even though the Rostovs' friend Marya Dmitrievna publicly calls her a whore.

After Borodino, Pierre is dazed and distressed, traveling on the road to Mozhaysk, where he intends to take refuge. Sleeping in the courtyard of an inn, he dreams of his Masonic benefactor and of other acquaintances. He awakens to news that Mozhaysk is being abandoned to the French, and that Andrew and Anatole Kuragin are dead. Arriving in Moscow, Pierre is summoned by Count Rostopchin, the local commander in chief. Another official tells Pierre of a case involving a forged Napoleonic proclamation, and also conveys rumors about Helene's plans to travel to Europe. Count Rostopchin warns Pierre to break off contact with the Masons. Informed that Helene has converted to Catholicism to attain a divorce, and reflecting sadly on Andrew's death, Pierre suddenly abandons the twelve people waiting to conduct business with him. He flees into the city of Moscow without telling anyone where he is going.

When Petya joins the hussars, Countess Rostova is distressed that both her sons may be killed at any moment. Meanwhile, the Rostov family inefficiently prepares to flee Moscow, despite contradictory official rumors that no one will be allowed to leave. The countess is pleased at Nicholas's news of a romantic interest in the wealthy Princess Mary. Even Sonya admits this development is a good prospect, and she appeases her grief by directing the evacuation of the Rostov household. Natasha and Petya, home on leave, are in high spirits, awaiting the extraordinary events to come.

The Rostov household is in disorder as the evacuation from Moscow grows imminent. Natasha, too distracted to help pack the family's belongings, invites wounded soldiers stationed outside to stay in the Rostov home. Petya learns that there will be a battle the next day. The countess is terrified, but Petya is excited. Natasha takes control of the packing, and the household prepares to leave the following day. Andrew shows up wounded and dying, and is given refuge in the Rostov home without the Rostovs' knowledge.

Moscow is thrown into confusion, as commodities are pricier and serfs are running away. Just before departing, the old count generously offers to unload some of his carts and use them to convey wounded soldiers, despite his wife's objections. Under Natasha's influence, the count finally orders all the family's possessions to be unloaded, and all the carts made available to the wounded. Sonya, told that Andrew is among the soldiers being conveyed, informs the countess, who worries about Natasha's reaction and hides this development from her.

On the way out of the city, Natasha glimpses Pierre on the street. They talk, and Pierre says he is staying in Moscow. Natasha wishes to stay with him. Pierre, depressed with news of Helene's intended remarriage, has been living in the house of his deceased Masonic advisor, Bazdeev. Pierre has been sorting through the books and papers Bazdeev left, and has disguised himself in peasant clothes and armed himself with a pistol for self-protection.

## Book Eleven, Chapters 10–16

Napoleon, meanwhile, is in the Poklonny Hills near Moscow, filled with pride that the great city will soon be his and imagining the high level of civilization he will bring to Russia. He prepares to meet with the elders of the city, to appoint a governor, and to conduct other business. But Napoleon is startled and insulted by the news that the elders have left Moscow, and that the city is full only of drunken mobs, like a hive without its queen bee. Some of the Russian troops being convoyed out of Moscow are tempted to escape and loot the abandoned shops, and it is hard to maintain order among them.

With the gentry and administrators gone, anarchy threatens the city, and murders proliferate.

Count Rostopchin, local commander of Moscow, is told to reinstate order. In order to promote public tranquility, however, he lies to the common folk, telling them Moscow is in no danger of French invasion. He also makes insufficient preparations for total evacuation of the city. Though out of touch with popular feeling, Rostopchin imagines himself as leader of the people of Moscow. When he is told to leave the city without any opportunity for heroism, his ego is wounded. He gives thoughtless orders to release prison inmates and patients from mental asylums out into the city.

Rostopchin prepares to leave Moscow, but he is delayed by the necessity of dealing with a political traitor named Vereshchagin—the man who earlier forged Napoleonic decrees and distributed them. Rostopchin publicly displays Vereshchagin and orders the crowd to punish him, which they do with cruelty. Inwardly, Rostopchin is sickened by the mob. Riding in his carriage on the way out of the city, he is approached by a lunatic who thinks himself to be Jesus Christ. Rostopchin again is inwardly appalled at the cruelty he has caused. Rostopchin meets Kutuzov, whom he gently blames for the chaos in Moscow. Kutuzov meaninglessly states that Moscow will not be abandoned without a battle, though that is exactly what is occurring. The French troops enter Moscow and delightedly enjoy its houses and food supplies, looting wherever they can. Careless soldiers contribute to igniting vast fires that consume much of the city.

Meanwhile, Pierre, still lodged in Bazdeev's house, is obsessed by what he sees as mystical evidence that he is destined to be Napoleon's vanquisher. Constantly drunk and nearly insane, he develops a fantastic plot to assassinate the French leader. When a French officer named Ramballe wanders into the house, Bazdeev's madman brother fires upon him. Pierre forgets his disguise and rushes to the officer's aid, asking him in French if he has been wounded. Ramballe calls Pierre his savior and invites him to dine. The patriotic Frenchman rhapsodizes about Paris and informs Pierre that Napoleon is to arrive the next day. He tells Pierre tales of love, and Pierre confesses his love for Natasha.

The Rostovs catch sight of Moscow in flames, which causes the countess and the servants to weep. Natasha, who has learned that Andrew is in their convoy, is agitated to think he is sleeping just across the courtyard. In the night, she sneaks into his room and greets him. For the first time, Andrew remembers his earlier battlefield revelation about true happiness. He imagines Natasha to be a hallucination at first, but then sees she is real. Natasha begs Andrew for forgiveness.

The half-crazed Pierre prepares his plans to assassinate Napoleon and goes out with a dagger under his cloak, walking in a dazed and distracted manner. As if waking up from a dream, he comes upon a burning house with a woman standing outside, weeping over a little girl left inside. Pierre circumvents the French guards, enters the house, and saves the girl. Once outside again, he is unable to find the girl's family. Then, attempting to stop a Frenchman from bothering an Armenian girl, Pierre becomes angry, attracting the attention of the French authorities, who arrest him on suspicions of espionage.

---

## Analysis: Book Eleven

The idea of renunciation, of surrendering the external valuables of one's life, recurs frequently in these chapters as Tolstoy's symbol of spiritual achievement. This renunciation is both private and public, both emotional and military. The citizens of Smolensk give up their city to the invading French, and Kutuzov follows suit by regretfully surrendering the city of Moscow. Such surrender astonishes Napoleon, who in his materialistic fashion cannot fathom that a country would prefer spiritual freedom to material loss of property. Indeed, we see that the Russian abandonment of Moscow is the real undoing of the French. The invaders loot Russian treasures, but they cannot conquer Russia. The French failure to conquer the Russian soul is mirrored on an individual level in Pierre, who, even when held captive, knows that the French cannot touch his "immortal soul." We see another willing surrender of the physical world in the Rostovs' abandonment of their possessions so that the wounded Russian soldiers may be evacuated from Moscow. To Tolstoy, giving up material possessions is not a loss, but rather a spiritual gain.

Tolstoy constantly emphasizes the absurdity of war in his portrayal of occupied Moscow through Pierre's eyes. Pierre's awareness of the stupidity of the war is heightened by the fact that, of the Russians, he is the one most symbolically associated with the French. Pierre is called by a French name throughout the novel (the narrator never calls him "Petr," as the name "Peter" typically appears in Russian), speaks French beautifully, has lived in Paris, and gets along well with the French officer Ramballe. Through Pierre's example, Tolstoy—himself one of the modern world's great pacifists and an important influence on Gandhi's doctrine of non-aggression—highlights the human instinct for solidarity and togetherness that opposes the contrary instinct for division and bloodshed.

## BOOKS TWELVE–THIRTEEN

### BOOK TWELVE

> *The proverbs, of which his talk was full, were . . .*
> *those folk sayings which taken without a context seem*
> *so insignificant, but when used appositely suddenly*
> *acquire a significance of profound wisdom.*
>
> (See QUOTATIONS, p. 72)

St. Petersburg high society continues its glittering life, almost unaware of the nation's sufferings. Helene has fallen ill and is being treated by an Italian doctor, though everyone knows her trouble results from her marital dilemma. At one of Anna Pavlovna's parties, Vasili Kuragin reads a solemn greeting to the tsar from a bishop, praying for military victory. Anna predicts that good news will arrive the next day, the tsar's birthday.

Indeed, the next day, a great deal of news breaks: the victory at Borodino, the deaths of several generals, and the sudden death of Helene, the result of a drug overdose. The tsar receives a letter from Rastopchin, recounting Kutuzov's decision to leave Moscow. The tsar writes to Kutuzov, expressing his great regret at this decision. Kutuzov responds with a messenger, Colonel Michaud, to tell the tsar of the burning of Moscow. The tsar tearfully vows to do everything possible to save his country and defeat Napoleon.

The narrator reminds us that even in such dire times, patriotism and heroism were still less important in people's lives than their own trivial, everyday, private interests. Nicholas, getting by like everyone else, travels to Voronezh to buy remounts for his regiments. After conducting his business, Nicholas attends a local governor's ball and flirts with another man's attractive wife. Then, Mary's aunt Malvintseva, who is also present, invites Nicholas to visit her and Mary. The governor's wife offers to arrange a marriage between Nicholas and Mary. Nicholas admits he is attracted to Mary, but says that he loves and is engaged to Sonya. The governor's wife counters that marrying Sonya would not be beneficial in the long run. The governor's wife's plan disturbs Mary, who is still overcome with grief about her father. Though Mary is worried about how to speak to Nicholas, she is nonetheless charming to him when he visits, and seems illuminated by love. Nicholas is attracted to Mary, but is confused by his promises to Sonya and by his inability to imagine being married to Mary. He is impressed by her moral seriousness, but also a bit scared of her.

Nicholas receives a letter from Sonya graciously ending her engagement with him and informing him that Natasha is nursing the wounded Andrew. Sonya has written the letter under pressure from Countess Rostova, who has demanded that Sonya repay her debts to the family by giving up Nicholas so he can marry Mary. Secretly, however, Sonya feels that Nicholas is destined to be hers. She reminds Natasha of her supposed vision of Andrew lying down, saying that the prophecy has come true, and implying that Natasha and Andrew are destined to be together.

Meanwhile, the French treat Pierre with hostile respect while they hold him captive on suspicions of espionage. Pierre feels sad when his captors make fun of him. The authorities try his case with a guilty verdict as a foregone conclusion. Pierre refuses to state his name, which annoys the French. They lead Pierre through the burning streets of Moscow to the office of the marshal, Davout. Pierre establishes a human connection with Davout, but is nonetheless led out to his execution. Pierre reflects that some kind of system beyond his understanding has condemned him to death. Pierre and five other prisoners are led into a field. The other prisoners are shot and buried by riflemen, some of whom are sickened by their crimes. Pierre is unexpectedly pardoned and taken as a prisoner to a dirty shed. Stupefied by the experience, Pierre does not understand what has happened. One of the other prisoners, Platon Karataev, impresses Pierre with his sincerity, simplicity, good sense, faith, and kindness to his dog. The middle-aged Platon never complains, and he treats everyone with unfailing good cheer.

Princess Mary, receiving news that the Rostovs are at Yaroslavl, sets off immediately to see her brother Andrew, who is with them. She arrives at the home where the Rostovs are staying, and the Countess greets her warmly. Natasha tearfully speaks to Mary about Andrew's condition. Natasha takes Mary into the room where Andrew is lying, and Mary is shocked to see her brother looking soft and gentle. Mary knows this appearance to be a sign of his approaching death. Andrew quietly tells Mary that fate has brought him together with Natasha after all. Andrew also speaks to Mary about Nicholas, giving his approval of their marriage. Mary prays to God for Andrew's soul. Andrew, aware he is dying, contemplates life and death. He confesses his love to Natasha, who cares for him tirelessly. Wavering between consciousness and oblivion, Andrew thinks of love as a unifying force, but he is aware that his ideas are cerebral and lack something. Under Natasha's and Mary's loving watch, Andrew dies.

### BOOK THIRTEEN

Kutuzov leads the Russian troops back toward Moscow, restraining them from attacking the vestiges of the French army. Napoleon writes an arrogant letter to Kutuzov from Moscow, which Kutuzov interprets as asking for settlements. The Russian army is rested and stronger than before, and is superior to the French forces in Moscow.

Kutuzov, with his characteristic genius of profiting from randomness, is aware that he cannot restrain his troops, so he orders an advance. Furious to discover that his orders are not received, he is forced to wait an extra day. During the battle, the Russian regiments are divided and confused as usual, and many men are killed pointlessly. One regiment fights well, however. Kutuzov, who is able to restrain his column from attacking, is decorated for the battle.

Napoleon inexplicably withdraws from Moscow, avoiding further battle engagements. Napoleon issues proclamations to the Muscovites assuring them that churches, theaters, and marketplaces are operating again, and that tranquility is returning to city life. None of these proclamations have any real effect, and the French loot the city as they depart.

Pierre spends a month ragged and barefoot in prison, respected by his captors and on friendly terms with a nameless dog. His fellow inmate Platon Karataev sews a shirt for a French officer and is forced to hand over the leftover scraps of cloth. The officer then feels guilty and gives the scraps back to Platon, who wants to use them as leg bandages. Surprisingly, in prison Pierre feels happy for the first time in his life, appreciating simple pleasures like food and sleep. He remembers Andrew's bitter comment that happiness is merely the absence of suffering. Pierre now agrees with Andrew's words—without the bitterness.

The French release the Russian prisoners and force them to march with the French troops in the evacuation of Moscow. During the march, Pierre and the soldiers are happy despite cruelty and privations on the part of the French. Pierre is aware of a mysterious force that protects him from physical suffering. He knows that the French cannot touch his immortal soul, regardless of what they do to his body.

The Russian officers Dokhturov and Konovnitsyn receive word that Napoleon is in Forminsk, and they pass this information on to Kutuzov. Kutuzov, still wondering whether Borodino has dealt a mortal wound to the French, receives the news gratefully, under-standing that Napoleon has left Moscow and that Russia is saved. As the French forces retreat back to Smolensk on their way to France, Kutuzov is unable to prevent Russian troops from attacking them.

---

### ANALYSIS: BOOKS TWELVE–THIRTEEN

The spiritual connection developing between Nicholas and Princess Mary in these chapters mirrors the deeply moving bond between Natasha and Andrew when they are reunited. In both cases Tolstoy emphasizes a profound spiritual union between a man and a woman that may have an erotic element, but that goes far beyond mere romantic love. Nicholas is unquestionably attracted to Mary, but his attraction is different from all his earlier dalliances with women, including his love for Sonya. With Mary, he feels more than simple pleasure or happiness, as he is struck by her moral earnestness and spiritual devotion. Similarly, Natasha's connection with Andrew, though once merely a romantic crush, now consists of a deeper caring and devotion, as she looks after her dying former fiancé. For both Rostov siblings, involvement with the spiritually serious Bolkonski family proves to be an emotional education. Both Nicholas and Natasha move beyond their earlier pursuits of romantic happiness and enter a more spiritually committed state.

Pierre's identity crisis as he wanders through occupied Moscow is a major turning point in the development of his character, and an important symbolic event in the novel overall. Pierre's identity has always been a bit uncertain, even from the beginning when he is introduced as a bastard child without any ensured inheritance. Educated abroad, Pierre feels like an outsider: he has awkward ways, his sincerity distinguishes him from the polished fakes of the Russian upper classes, and even his body looks different. This sense of being an outcast reaches its culmination when Pierre, watching Moscow burn, asks who he is. This uncertain identity, however, is also a source of power for Pierre. His refusal to tell his French captors his name comes across as an act of heroism rather than of cowardice, and his nameless status earns him notoriety in the prison camp. Being nameless forces him to focus inwardly on questions of inner happiness, and indeed Pierre finds himself happier in prison than ever before—just as the prison dog, called by several different names, is happy being unidentified. Identity is social and external, while happiness is internal only.

Pierre, one of the novel's more innocent characters, simply cannot understand the cruelty he witnesses. Taken as prisoner before the French marshal, he feels a momentary awareness of common human brotherhood with the man, and is reassured that this feeling will prove stronger than the dictates of war. But Pierre is wrong, as the Frenchman quickly regains his belief that the French and Russians are enemies, ordering Pierre to be executed. The execution of the five prisoners, which Pierre witnesses in a state of trauma, is utterly unexplainable and unjustifiable to his simple heart. The killing is objectionable even to the French executioners, who appear ashamed of their actions, especially the one of them who swoons when it is over.

Platon Karataev is one of the most celebrated characters in *War and Peace*. His qualities have been trumpeted not only by earlier Soviet critics who saw in him the best of the Russian peasant virtues, but also by foreigners who have seen him as a figure of unparalleled vitality. Platon's fame is surprising, as he appears in only a dozen pages of this vast novel. But he appears at a critical moment, during Pierre's lapse into misery, confusion, and existential anguish in prison. Platon shows up as a beacon of hope simply because he needs so little to be happy, demonstrating to Pierre that happiness is separate from all external factors, including health and freedom. Platon bustles busily around the prison, talking to the dog, sewing a shirt for a French officer, and quoting Russian proverbs at key moments. His first name is the Russian name for Plato, the Greek philosopher who counseled us to look beyond the material world to a realm of greater peace and certainty. Platon, though an illiterate man who has probably never heard of Plato, illustrates the philosopher's life-affirming teachings.

# BOOKS FOURTEEN–FIFTEEN

## BOOK FOURTEEN

The narrator again expresses his view that war is not scientific, repeating that the French defeat in Russia is rationally unexplainable. He then describes the devastation of the remaining French troops by Russian guerillas.

Dolokhov and Denisov are among the Cossack partisan fighters tracking the retreating French. Denisov receives a message delivered by Petya Rostov, who is now proudly serving in the army. Denisov and Petya come upon a French encampment and consider attacking it. Suddenly, they see a Russian peasant fleeing the French camp, whom Denisov recognizes as Tikhon, a feisty character who enjoys looting the French soldiers. Tikhon is sent off to capture a French informer, but kills the first Frenchman he finds on grounds that his clothes are not fancy enough. Denisov is disgusted by Tikhon's cruelty. Petya, eager to please Denisov, acts kindly toward a French drummer boy the Russians have taken prisoner. Petya hopes to take part in the attack on the French camp planned for the next day, and is finally allowed to do so.

Dolokhov and Petya, disguised as French officers, enter the French camp for information about Russian prisoners of war. Back at the Russian guerilla camp, Petya is unable to sleep before the battle, so he goes out to speak to a Cossack who sharpens Petya's saber. Petya feels as though he is in a dream. When the battle begins, the overjoyed Petya rides with glee into the heart of the shooting. He is killed.

Entering the French camp, Dolokhov and Denisov liberate the Russian prisoners of war, including Pierre, who had been marching painfully with the French while his friend Platon Karataev grew more and more ill. One day, Platon had told a tale of a merchant who suffered for the sins of others and greeted death happily. The next day, the French had shot Platon for being ill and straggling behind the rest. When Dolokhov and Denisov release Pierre, he weeps with joy. Petya is buried.

The French army continues to disintegrate. The troops fight among themselves and plunder each other. Napoleon abandons his subordinates. Nevertheless, Russians readers of histories of the war are frustrated to note that the Russian forces were unable to destroy the remnants of the French army. The narrator explains that attacking the retreating French would have been senseless, like whipping an animal already running.

## BOOK FIFTEEN

Mary and Natasha, still in exile from Moscow, grieve Andrew's death in silence and pain. Natasha is much changed, and she refuses to return to Moscow even when the danger is past. She receives word that her brother Petya is dead, and tells her mother, both weeping. Mary attempts to console Natasha, who grows so pale and thin that her father insists that she accompany Mary to Moscow to see doctors.

Unable to pursue the retreating French effectively, Kutuzov is accused of blundering in 1812—a view shared by many historians. The narrator disagrees with this opinion, considering Kutuzov an unsung hero. The Russian troops are in excellent spirits, singing and dancing despite the wretched conditions. Two exhausted French officers emerge from the forest, one of them Ramballe, whom Pierre saved earlier. The Russians give the Frenchmen food and drink.

General Kutuzov, meanwhile, goes to Vilna for rest and recovery. The tsar meets him and, despite criticism of Kutuzov's military maneuvers, awards him the highest state honors. The tsar wishes to continue the war, but Kutuzov objects, citing the impossibility of levying fresh troops. Kutuzov is replaced as military commander, and later dies.

After reaching safety, Pierre falls ill for three months. After his recovery, he reminisces about the events of the war, including the deaths of Petya and Andrew. He gradually understands that he will no longer be ordered anywhere, that food is available, and that his wife and the French are no longer threats to him. He is no longer obsessed by questions about the meaning of life, but simply accepts life as its own meaning, in accordance with God's will. Everyone notices that Pierre has become simpler after his ordeal. His estate manager informs him that the burning of Moscow has cost Pierre two million rubles, but that if Pierre does not rebuild, he could come out ahead financially. Pierre muses that loss has made him richer. Meanwhile, Muscovites return to their city, making it even more populous by 1813 than it was before the war. Pierre returns to his house in Moscow. He visits Princess Mary in her house when a lady in black is there also, and only after much time has passed does he realize the lady is Natasha. Pierre understands immediately that he loves Natasha.

Mary, Natasha, and Pierre speak of the deaths of Andrew and Petya, and Pierre says that faith is necessary to accept such losses. With Pierre present, Natasha is able to share deep feelings about Andrew she has never spoken of before. Pierre tells of his adventures in Moscow, and Mary contemplates the possibility of love between Natasha and Pierre. Afterward, Natasha and Mary privately talk about Pierre, and Mary calls him splendid and morally improved after his ordeal.

The next day, Pierre realizes he loves Natasha and must be her husband. He is full of goodwill toward everyone, and even finds Moscow's ruins beautiful. Pierre goes to visit Mary and Natasha for dinner again, staying later than he should and telling them he plans to remain in Moscow. Privately, Mary tells Pierre that he has a chance of winning Natasha, but that it is best that he leave Moscow for the present. Pierre is deliriously happy. Natasha is likewise overcome with joy when Mary tells her what Pierre has said.

---

## ANALYSIS: BOOKS FOURTEEN–FIFTEEN

Tolstoy's attitude toward the war as a Russian writer comes across clearly in these chapters. He attributes the final Russian victory over Napoleon and the withdrawal of French troops to Russia's spiritual greatness, but he does not narrate with patriotism. However, the narrator spares no praise in describing the Muscovites who leave behind their possessions rather than submit to foreign occupation. Likewise, he praises the way in which Kutuzov leads his troops with Russian soulful sensitivity rather than French logic. Furthermore, the narrator's portrait of Platon Karataev's peasant virtues is a clear tribute to the Russian countryside. Yet Tolstoy does not exaggerate Russian virtues, and he also reveals to us the dark side of the Russian war experience. The grim episode in which the peasant guerilla Tikhon needlessly kills a potential French prisoner of war shows us the cruelty of which the Russian peasant is capable. By the same token, the shocking death of Petya Rostov reminds us that even successful wars of defense—even ones that save Russia—bring needless and tragic deaths. Tolstoy shows the war to have been useful and good, but he does not revel in it patriotically or uncritically.

Pierre's reaction to the killing of Platon Karataev shows us the deep reserves of selfless sympathy that help define his character. Pierre had hardly known Platon long, but the loss is traumatic to him, and he is unable to bring himself to watch the shooting. The howling of the little dog communicates all we need to know about the devastation of this loss for Pierre, which affects him almost on an animal level. The vision of Platon returns to Pierre later during his recuperation, proving again his extraordinary connection with this unknown Russian peasant. Pierre's ability to forge deep emotional connections with strangers forms a striking contrast with Napoleon, who shows no emotional connections even with those near him. The narrator makes a point of emphasizing how Napoleon took a warm fur coat for himself during the French retreat, riding off alone and abandoning his troops and officers. French individualism is portrayed in a strongly negative light, the opposite of the Russian tendency for warm human relations.

Natasha and Pierre's sudden love is one of the most surprising developments in *War and Peace*. Pierre's first wife, Helene, is nothing like Natasha, and he finds nothing but disappointment in their marriage. Natasha has been in love with several men by this point; her feelings toward Pierre have always been warm but not romantic. Yet, in another sense, this love almost seems predestined and inevitable. Natasha and Pierre are the two most emotionally sincere and profound characters in the novel, both of them displaying a childlike openness toward the world that neither of their earlier respective love interests, Andrew or Helene, had. Natasha and Pierre share a sensitivity and depth that make them perfect emotional matches for each other. Moreover, both of them have suffered enormously in the past year, enduring extraordinary personal losses that have forced them both to turn inward and reevaluate the meaning of life. They are both ready for a renewal, and their love is perfectly timed. The fact that their relationship develops under the supervision of the morally wise Mary gives a kind of validity and sanctity to it, a sense that their love has been blessed.

# FIRST EPILOGUE–SECOND EPILOGUE

### FIRST EPILOGUE

The narrator examines historians' attitudes toward Tsar Alexander and Napoleon, finding them once again oversimplified, and asserts again the view that history is made not by great men, but by countless tiny factors.

Natasha and Pierre are married in 1813. Count Rostov dies that same year, after seeking his family's forgiveness for ruining their finances. Nicholas, who is in Paris when he receives the news, accepts his inheritance, which amounts to debts totaling twice the value of the deceased count's property. Nicholas pays what he can, borrowing money from Pierre, and enters government service to pay the rest of the debts. Nicholas struggles to maintain his mother and Sonya in their customary luxury, hiding his poverty from them.

Mary arrives in Moscow, having heard reports that Nicholas is sacrificing himself for his mother. Nicholas is unexpectedly cold to Mary. Countess Rostova presses Nicholas to court Mary. After a long silence, Nicholas visits Mary, treating her formally. Mary tells him that she misses the man she used to know, but that she accepts his new attitude. Secretly she still feels love, and starts crying. Suddenly they both realize a relationship is possible between them.

The year 1813 also sees the marriage of Nicholas and Mary. Nicholas soon repays all his debts and becomes a successful, traditional Russian farmer who takes special interest in his peasants. He rebuilds Bald Hills. Despite occasional antagonism, Nicholas and Mary are a happily married couple. Nicholas reads Mary's parenting journal, in which she records her child-rearing experiments, such as grading her children on their behavior. Nicholas approves of Mary's enthusiasm as a mother, though he somewhat objects to her pedantic style. Nicholas criticizes Natasha's domination of Pierre without realizing that he dominates Mary in the same way. Mary tries to be patient, listening to her husband's financial updates while striving to maintain Christian forbearance and forgiveness.

By 1820, Natasha has become a sturdy mother of four, thinking only of her family, never of fashions or accomplishments. Pierre wholly submits to his role as family man, never flirting with women or dining out. When Pierre overstays a trip to St. Petersburg by three weeks, Natasha becomes worried and irritable, but then is filled with joy when he returns with gifts for the family. Pierre discusses St. Petersburg gossip with his family and with his friend Denisov, who has accompanied him home.

Andrew's fifteen-year-old son, Nicholas Bolkonski, adores Pierre and wants to stay up late to be with him. Pierre speaks to young Nicholas about the problems of running charitable institutions. Pierre asserts that things are rotten in St. Petersburg, predicting an overthrow soon. Privately, Natasha and Pierre reflect on their home life and whether Platon Karataev would have approved of it. Pierre concludes that the peasant would have, though he hesitates somewhat in his response. Nicholas Bolkonski muses on his veneration for his uncle Pierre, and dreams of military glory.

## SECOND EPILOGUE

After further musings on the enigma of history in the abstract and philosophical Second Epilogue, the narrator reflects on human power. Power, which he defines as the collective will of the people transferred to one ruler, is the only identifiable motor that drives history forward. But power is impossible to define, so the mystery of history is insoluble. It is impossible to explain why Napoleon, for example, despite a repeatedly expressed desire to invade England, never took any steps to do so, but instead invaded Russia, a country he wanted as an ally.

The enigma of historical change implies the theological question about free will and the extent to which any individual is truly free in his actions, whatever his illusions of freedom may be. According to the narrator, it is just as impossible to imagine total freedom as it is to imagine total determinism. In the end, the narrator puts forth the idea that we must necessarily depend on a power of which we are not conscious. This idea amounts to a recognition that, though our sense of freedom is indispensable, so too is our repressed understanding that we are part of something bigger than ourselves, a force that moves our lives forward.

---

## ANALYSIS: FIRST EPILOGUE–SECOND EPILOGUE

The fortunes of the Rostov family continue their fluctuations, but end on an optimistic upswing that bodes well for the future of Russia. Despite Tolstoy's presentation of Nicholas as an honorable son making sacrifices for his family, the author allows room for a bit of criticism. The same aristocratic disregard for money matters that ruined the Rostovs is still present and still harmful, as we see in the fact that Nicholas suffers so his mother can continue her financially oblivious lifestyle. Yet we still sense there is hope for the future. Mary's love ensures that Nicholas and his family are saved financially and suggests that better fortunes are fated for the future of Russia as a whole. It is important that enrichment comes from spiritual sources such as love rather than from economic ones—Nicholas does not consider going into trade. Nicholas's new wealth is like manna from heaven rather than the fruits of enterprise. In his farm management, Nicholas is not interested in new western agricultural science, but shows a markedly traditionalist attitude toward his land that aligns him with his own Russian peasants more than with modern western landowners. Tolstoy thus hints that Russia can prosper as Nicholas prospers, despite a history of profligacy and waste, while still remaining true to his Russian traditions.

Readers who make it to the end of the novel often complain about the abstract dryness of the Second Epilogue, which reads more like a treatise on the philosophy of history than the conclusion of an absorbing piece of fiction. Yet the Second Epilogue, while undeniably difficult, is essential to understanding Tolstoy's deepest meanings in *War and Peace*. Here, the author's obsession with the irrationality of history throughout more than a thousand pages of the novel becomes relevant to more than just our ability to grasp what takes place on the field at Borodino. History is not simply an interpretation of events, but an investigation of their true causes—which, in Tolstoy's explanation, is ultimately God. We finally see here that the question of history's inexplicability is really a question of theology, individual free will, and our ability to judge our ownership of our actions and our lives.

Our unconscious dependence on hidden forces, the idea with which Tolstoy ends his mammoth novel, is really a final tribute to God's secret laws, which are inscrutable to human minds. This inscrutable truth is seen not merely in wartime events like the inexplicable Russian victory over the French, but in personal events like Nicholas's sudden and unexpected decision to wed Mary. Though this marriage initially seems just as irrational as Napoleon's defeat at Borodino, in the end we sense that it is just as fated, and therefore yet another component of God's mysterious, higher plan for human history.

# IMPORTANT QUOTATIONS EXPLAINED

1. "Well, Prince, so Genoa and Lucca are now just family estates of the Buonapartes. But I warn you, if you don't tell me that this means war, if you still try to defend the infamies and horrors perpetrated by that Antichrist—I really believe he is Antichrist—I will have nothing more to do with you. . . ."

These words from the St. Petersburg society hostess Anna Pavlovna Scherer brilliantly open *War and Peace* in Book One, Chapter 1, establishing a dual focus on the wartime idea of Napoleonic aggression and the peacetime idea of conversation at a high-society party. These lines immediately attune us to the fact that war and peace are constantly interwoven in the novel, as military maneuvers go hand in hand with socializing. Anna Pavlovna is surprisingly well informed about current events, a far cry from the somewhat insulated mindset we might expect from such a socialite. The Italian principalities of Genoa and Lucca are far from St. Petersburg, yet Anna Pavlovna has a global view of their importance, just as a minister of war might have. Her toughness in addressing the prince, with threatening phrases such as "I warn you" and "I will have nothing more to do with you," shows that she is ready to act like a general—a trait we also see in her dictatorial way of running her party. Moreover, Anna Pavlovna shows a diplomat's sensitivity to the political subtleties of language, as when she calls Napoleon by his Italian name, Buonaparte, rather than his French name, Bonaparte, thereby delicately insulting Napoleon's non-French background.

Yet if Anna Pavlovna introduces the prospect of war into the novel, she also reveals how arbitrary and absurd people's understanding of war often is, both on and off the battlefield. Her declaration that Napoleon is the Antichrist comes across as exaggerated and ridiculous, especially in light of later developments, when we see Tolstoy's portrait of the French emperor as a silly, vainglorious, and deluded little man. Napoleon may be dangerous, but he is hardly the principal of evil incarnate. Similarly, Anna Pavlovna's threats to the prince are social games, not intended seriously or taken seriously. As such, we feel that most talk of war in higher state circles may be similarly blustery and hollow. Anna Pavlovna may only be feigning an interest in the war to appear current and informed. We do not detect much real emotion in what she says, even though the war may well threaten her own country's well being. Moreover, Anna Pavlovna makes no effort to argue against the prince's supposed defense of Napoleon by appealing to reason or evidence. Instead, she does so merely through a trivial threat that she will no longer speak to the prince if he holds to his opinions. Reason and clear judgment appear to have little validity in discussions about war, as Tolstoy repeatedly shows throughout the novel.

2.    Pierre, who from the moment Prince Andrew entered
      the room had watched him with glad, affectionate
      eyes, now came up and took his arm. Before he looked
      round Prince Andrew frowned again, expressing his
      annoyance with whoever was touching his arm, but
      when he saw Pierre's beaming face he gave him an
      unexpectedly kind and pleasant smile.

This early picture of Pierre and Andrew from Book One, Chapter 1, shows us a great deal about the characters of both men. We see that Pierre views the prospect of greeting Andrew with sincere and simple pleasure, his "glad, affectionate" eyes showing a nearly canine joy in making contact with someone he likes. Tolstoy thus presents Pierre to us as a deeply social person who thrives on human connection. Andrew, by contrast, instinctively dislikes human contact and is not ashamed to show this detachment, "expressing his annoyance with whoever was touching his arm." Andrew does not like being touched, though in the case of Pierre he makes an exception to his rule and returns Pierre's show of affection. It is not that Andrew secretly dislikes Pierre, but rather that Andrew's instinct is to avoid human contact, whereas Pierre's instinct is to pursue it.

When broadly applied to the lives of these two men, this contrast in attitudes toward human contact shows us much about how the men live and the choices they make. Pierre jumps all too eagerly into human contact when, in Helene, he makes a disastrous choice of a wife. However, the identity crisis that follows from Helene's deception of him pushes him on a search for wisdom. Pierre ends the novel happily married, having apparently learned from his earlier mistakes in forging the wrong kind of connections with people. Andrew, by contrast, is alone at the end of the novel, unmarried to the woman he loves seemingly because he insisted on following his father's wish in delaying the marriage—but perhaps really because he secretly feared starting another relationship. Both Andrew and Pierre arrive at surprising and life-changing realizations that they love Natasha, but Andrew remains alone and untouched in the end, while Pierre is able to forge a union with her. In this regard, this early scene with the two men prefigures larger, more significant developments that occur much later in the novel.

3.   This black-eyed, wide-mouthed girl, not pretty but full
     of life . . . ran to hide her flushed face in the lace of her
     mother's mantilla—not paying the least attention to
     her severe remark—and began to laugh. She laughed,
     and in fragmentary sentences tried to explain about a
     doll which she produced from the folds of her frock.

This passage from Book One, Chapter 5, introduces the major female character in *War and Peace*, the twelve-year-old Natasha Rostova, in a manner that reveals to us much of the symbolic importance she has in the novel as a whole. Significantly, while almost all the other main characters are introduced by name before they are physically described, Natasha is left nameless for some time. She appears at first less an individual human being than a mythic presence, an embodiment of vital girlhood "full of life." Her wide mouth suggests a readiness to feed on experiences and an eagerness to express herself fully, though not necessarily in any rational way. Natasha's inability to "explain" about her doll suggests that her soul is emotional rather than analytical. She may express herself through laughter, or other nonverbal means, better than she can by reasoning things out. Indeed, this emotional extravagance and rational limitation on Natasha's part continue to be evident long after she grows up, as we see when she submits to the seductive Anatole and plans a madcap elopement with him.

We also see Natasha's bold and even rebellious spirit clearly here in her indifference to the stern remarks from her mother. Parental threats mean nothing to Natasha: she will do what she will do, with little care for what the authorities or elders say. The Rostov family friend Marya Dmitrievna sees this rebellious spirit in Natasha when she nicknames her "the Cossack," a name that, in its fondness, suggests that Natasha's rebelliousness is a quality to be appreciated and perhaps even admired. This rebellion, however, leads to unhappiness later, as when Natasha braves Sonya's criticism and her family's disapproval in planning to elope with the roguish Anatole. But in the end, we feel that this trait leads Natasha to a deeper wisdom than a scrupulous rule-abider like Sonya could ever attain. Finally, Natasha's clutching of a beloved baby doll in these lines foreshadows her ultimate role as mother of four. She hides in her mother's mantilla holding her imagined child, suggesting a strong bond between grandmother, mother, and child that underscores the values of the Rostov family and the continuity of their line.

4.  When everything was ready, the stranger opened his eyes, moved to the table, filled a tumbler with tea for himself and one for the beardless old man to whom he passed it. Pierre began to feel a sense of uneasiness, and the need, even the inevitability, of entering into conversation with this stranger.

In this passage, from Book Five, Chapter 1, Pierre is waiting at the Torzhok station for a connection on his way to St. Petersburg, having just left his wife after discovering she has been cheating on him with his friend. Pierre is bitter and depressed, and as he waits mindlessly he meets a mysterious old man with a strange servant—two figures who, in their dreamlike, almost surreal quality, contrast with the realistic normalcy of most characters in *War and Peace*. The old man wears a ring with a death's head on it, and he sits in total Zen-like silence for a long time. His servant appears to have no beard, not because he has recently shaved but because no beard has ever grown. The slightly androgynous, sexless quality of both men inevitably affects Pierre, who has just been punished, in effect, for marrying the wrong woman as a result of sexual passion. The two men may unconsciously represent a freedom from the impulses of sex, and therefore a liberation of the spirit. It is precisely a spiritual rebirth for which Pierre yearns in his present misery. As we see with Pierre always, he seeks spiritual rebirth not through introspection or books alone, but through a connection with people. Consequently, even though these two men make Pierre "uneasy," he does not avoid them, as Andrew would likely do, but rather feels it inevitable that he will interact with them and gain something from them.

Although the first stranger mentioned appears to be the master of the beardless man who is the servant, it is nevertheless the first man who pours a glass of tea for the beardless man. While the servant later does perform tasks for his master, this initial tea ceremony is somewhat symbolic, creating an environment of social equality. This hint of a leveling of social ranks may unconsciously appeal to Pierre, whose most important influence later in the novel comes not from a tsar, prince, or emperor, but from a simple and humble Russian peasant, Platon Karataev. The two strangers may thus also represent an ideal of a classless society, or at least an ideal of a strong, comradely connection between individuals of different classes.

QUOTATIONS

5.   When he related anything it was generally some old
     and evidently precious memory of his "Christian" life,
     as he called his peasant existence. The proverbs, of
     which his talk was full, were . . . those folk sayings
     which taken without a context seem so insignificant,
     but when used appositely suddenly acquire a
     significance of profound wisdom.

This description of the personality and behavior of the remarkable peasant Platon Karataev, from Book Twelve, Chapter 3, demonstrates how Tolstoy and Pierre both find Platon's ordinary and uneducated "insignificance" highly significant. Platon is exceptional in being so common, in the best sense of the word—part of the common or shared native traditions of Russia. Many members of the cultural elite of Tolstoy's day would have viewed Platon's liberal use of Russian proverbs as a sign of low-class status and illiteracy. Tolstoy, however, gives Platon's colloquial expression a mighty stamp of approval in referring to its "profound wisdom." This comment reveals much about the view of wisdom Tolstoy offers in *War and Peace*. Wisdom is not to be found in high culture or foreign culture—Andrew and Pierre both return from trips to Europe without having become noticeably wiser—but rather from the experience of what is right under our noses. Tolstoy implies that sometimes the wisdom of a very common proverb can go completely overlooked until the right speaker uses the proverb appropriately and suddenly imbues it with deep meaning.

This passage also reveals another important idea in the novel, the suggestion that truth and meaning lie in human beings and in the full experience of human life, rather than in detached ideas or images or doctrines. The narrator does not give us any examples of mind-boggling ideas Platon has put forth, but instead refers to "some old and evidently precious memory" that the peasant narrates. It is not clear that the memory is at all precious in and of itself, but only that it is "evidently" precious to Platon himself. This distinction is key. Tolstoy implies that it does not really matter what a memory is, but only that someone attaches a personal meaning to it in his own particular way. That meaning then infuses the person with such a glow of wisdom that anyone who hears him cannot help but be affected by it— as we see in the fact that Platon profoundly affects Pierre. The truth that strikes Pierre is not a single idea he can carry away with him, but rather the fuller experience of knowing and interacting with Platon and appreciating the meaning he is able to convey.

# KEY FACTS

FULL TITLE
*War and Peace* or *Voyna i mir*

AUTHOR
Lev (Leo) Nikolaevich Tolstoy

TYPE OF WORK
Novel

GENRE
Historical novel; realist novel; epic

LANGUAGE
Russian

TIME AND PLACE WRITTEN
1863–1869; the estate of Yasnaya Polyana, near Moscow

DATE OF FIRST PUBLICATION
1865–1869 (serial publication)

PUBLISHER
M.N. Katkov

NARRATOR
An unnamed, omniscient, detached, third-person narrator

POINT OF VIEW
The anonymous narrator presents facts and inner thoughts of characters that no single character in the novel could know all at once. The narrator describes characters' states of mind, feelings, and attitudes, as well as practical facts more relevant to a military historian. He also slides into philosophy in places, most notably in the second epilogue.

TONE
The narrator consistently maintains the impersonal but sympathetic tone most often used by the European realist novelists of the mid-nineteenth century. He focuses on facts and feelings with equal attentiveness, but allows himself few authorial commentaries on the fates of characters or editorial observations about the story unfolding. The bulk of his direct

authorial appearances are limited to musings on the philosophy of history sprinkled throughout the text. Generally, the description of a given scene is carefully detailed, again in general accordance with literary realism. This detailed realism underscores a point frequently made in the philosophical sections of the narrative, which is that little things and little people matter more than big ideas and great leaders.

TENSE
Past

SETTING (TIME)
1805–1820

SETTING (PLACE)
Various locations throughout Russia and eastern Europe, including St. Petersburg, Moscow, Austria, Prussia, the Russian eastern frontier, and Smolensk

PROTAGONISTS
Pierre Bezukhov; Andrew Bolkonski; Natasha Rostova; General Kutuzov; Mary Bolkonskaya; Nicholas Rostov

MAJOR CONFLICT
Napoleon's French forces triumphantly spread across Europe and threaten the balance of power that includes Russia; Russia responds by declaring war against France and fighting at the decisive Battle of Borodino. On the level of individual characters, Pierre, Andrew, Mary, Nicholas, and Natasha all grope their way through life while struggling to maintain their ideals, vitality, and love for humanity in the face of loss, sadness, and disillusionment.

RISING ACTION
Napoleon's conquests in western Europe, which alarm Russians with a threat of invasion; Pierre's inheritance, leaving him prey to schemers such as Helene Kuragina, who prompt his search for wisdom; Natasha's growth to womanhood, forcing her to choose a fitting mate; the testing of Mary's faith by a cruel world; the testing of Nicholas's heroic impulses by the limitations of his life; Andrew's loneliness after his wife's death, leading him to reevaluate the purpose of his life.

KEY FACTS

CLIMAX

The Russian troops' showdown with the French at the decisive Battle of Borodino; Pierre's meeting with Platon Karataev, who infuses him with wisdom; Natasha's parting with Andrew and bonding with Pierre; Mary's parting with her father and meeting with Nicholas

FALLING ACTION

The Russian victory at Borodino; the subsequent French withdrawal from Russia; the return to normalcy and everyday life for the Russians; Pierre's marriage to Natasha; Nicholas's marriage to Mary

THEMES

The irrationality of human motives; the search for the meaning of life; the limitations of leadership

MOTIFS

Inexplicable love; financial loss; death as a revelation

SYMBOLS

The Battle of Borodino; the French occupation of Moscow; Nicholas's rebuilding of Bald Hills

FORESHADOWING

Anna Pavlovna's prophecy of war against Napoleon later comes true when war is declared; Sonya's vision of Andrew lying down foreshadows Andrew's lying wounded on the field of Austerlitz and then lying as an invalid in the Rostov home; Natasha's first appearance with a doll foreshadows her later role as a mother.

# STUDY QUESTIONS & ESSAY TOPICS

## STUDY QUESTIONS

1.  War and Peace *is a historical novel. Tolstoy made great efforts to ensure the accuracy of his facts and dates, and the characters of Tsar Alexander I, Napoleon, Speranski, and other dignitaries generally respect historical factuality. Yet almost all the important and interesting characters in the novel are fictional. Why does Tolstoy merge fact and fiction in this fashion?*

The short answer is that historical novels *always* merge fact and fiction, as the contradictory terms "historical" and "novel" remind us. But the deeper and more interesting answer as to why Tolstoy chose a historical context for this particular story—unlike his later *Anna Karenina,* which is completely fictional—involves his complex theory of history. As Tolstoy repeatedly shows us in *War and Peace,* historians do not give us the whole truth about what happened on the battlefield, or anywhere else for that matter. They give us only their particular slant on what happened, distorted by their own prejudices, interpretations, and fantasies. The historian is, then, much more akin to a creative writer than he would likely admit. By writing an account of Napoleon's war with Russia from the Russian perspective, which had not yet been attempted at the time of the novel's publication (or so Tolstoy tells us), Tolstoy is suggesting that a fictional work may do the job of recording history just as well. Literature may tell the truth as effectively as supposedly objective history books that are in fact not objective at all.

Moreover, fiction has the power to reconstruct the lowly figures of history that the historian must necessarily leave out, as history itself forgets small individuals in its focus on great men and great leaders. Tolstoy's philosophy of history insists that great men are illusions, and that the high and the low alike are swept along by networks of circumstances. Therefore, he has a vested interest in depicting the significance of nobodies like Platon Karataev or

Pierre's executed prison mates. History books may be forced to overlook these small figures, but the novelist has the power to conjure them up before our eyes, to restore their rightful importance in the overall scheme of things.

2. *Early in the novel, Tolstoy takes great care in depicting two pairs of childhood sweethearts: Nicholas and Sonya, and Natasha and Boris. As the love stories in the novel are key, we expect these two relationships to blossom and develop over time, and to culminate finally in marriage. Yet oddly, neither does. Why does Tolstoy set up these two pairs so carefully, only to drive them apart in the end?*

Tolstoy indeed values love and courtship, which in *War and Peace* appear just as important in the overall scheme of things as battles and diplomacy. The choice of spouses is a very serious matter for Tolstoy, a philosophical statement about who one is and what one wants out of life. Pierre's greatest disappointment in life, for instance, his greatest spur to find the positive meaning in existence, is his bad decision to marry Helene. Tolstoy emphasizes that a good partner is a prerequisite not just for contentment at home, but for fulfillment as a person overall. Precisely for this reason, he emphasizes how characters' choices of mates change over time as their personalities develop and their lives unfold.

If Nicholas married Sonya at the end, and Natasha wedded Boris, the novel would suggest that the growth of these four characters has led them all full circle, back to their childhood crushes and early fantasies. At the opening of the novel, Nicholas is a boy full of illusions who loses forty-three thousand rubles in a card game, but by the end he is supporting his mother on a meager salary. He has changed greatly, and it is inevitable that his criteria for a good wife have changed as well. Similarly, at the beginning, Natasha is a mere girl who becomes attached to Boris partly in imitation of her cousin Sonya's attachment to Nicholas. Such love is child's play, an early romantic infatuation. But after the loss of her home and the death of her fiancé, Natasha understands that life is no game, but rather is full of pain and suffering. Boris, even in adulthood, does not appear to have suffered much, but Pierre has. In this regard, Tolstoy implies that Natasha's union with Pierre is a merging of spirits who have matured in the same direction over time.

3. *Tolstoy was fully aware that Napoleon's 1812 invasion of Russia would be a subject dear to the hearts of patriotic Russian readers. Though* War and Peace *depicts a Russian victory, the novel is not nearly as patriotic as it could be. Indeed, at times Tolstoy even makes an effort to downplay the patriotic dimension of his story. Why does he choose a historical moment brimming with nationalistic potential, but then refuse to trumpet a patriotic message?*

Tolstoy was certainly aware that the events of 1812 would, for a Russian reader, hold great patriotic significance. Russia had been under the sway of French culture for more than a century, to the extent that some Russian noblemen—like Prince Golitsyn mentioned in the novel—only spoke French, and could not even speak the Russian language. Economically, diplomatically, and culturally, France had been deemed superior to Russia for so long that a war between the two nations raised profound questions about who Russians really were, and whether they had a culture of their own. In the 1860s, when Tolstoy wrote *War and Peace,* this topic was a subject of hot debate between two groups in Russian intellectual society. The Westernizers believed that Russia should continue looking to Europe for guidance, whereas the Slavophiles argued that Russia should drop the West as a role model and follow its own unique path instead. The war between western Europe and Russia in Tolstoy's novel plays out this cultural conflict dramatically. The final victory for the Russians had a timely meaning for many readers and critics in the context of the 1860s, symbolizing hope for Russian cultural independence. The fact that the greatest moral voice in the novel is a Russian peasant, Platon Karataev, points to Tolstoy's interest in affirming native Russian folk wisdom.

Yet, as Tolstoy never ceases to point out in *War and Peace,* history is never simple, but is composed of inextricable networks of tightly linked factors. Indeed, the French and Russians are bound too closely to be fully separated. Platon is Russian, but perhaps Pierre would not have grasped the peasant's genius if he had not read so many French books and lived in Paris. Tolstoy emphasizes the interconnection between France and Russia in his insistence on consistently calling Pierre by his French name, never by his Russian name, Petr—even though other characters are named in both French and Russian (Anatole addresses Natasha as Natalie, for example). Tolstoy may be subtly pointing out that even people as appreciative of Russian culture as Pierre is have been indelibly marked by French culture. Tolstoy thus implies that cultural interdependence is inevitable, and not necessarily detrimental. Patriotism, meanwhile, requires precisely the opposite belief: that one national group must be wholly separated from another, and that they must be pitted against each other. Tolstoy values the notion of interconnected humanity, and the deep brotherhood of all humankind, too much to indulge in patriotic divisions.

## SUGGESTED ESSAY TOPICS

1. Why is Pierre initially satisfied with Freemasonry as a framework for meaning in his life, but then ultimately disappointed? What does Pierre's later spiritual development provide that the Masons could not offer?

2. Andrew seems to love Natasha genuinely, yet he obeys his father by waiting a year to marry. Andrew's duty to respect his father's wishes does not seem to fully explain his decision, as he defies his father on other occasions. Does Andrew use his father's command as an excuse for stalling Natasha? If so, why is Andrew conflicted about marrying her?

3. Tolstoy characterizes General Kutuzov as an admirable leader who is wise, devout, humble, and patient. But near the end of *War and Peace*, Kutuzov loses support and is widely criticized. Why does Tolstoy make this great leader into a neglected and unappreciated figure at the end of the novel?

4. Though the Kuragin family is highly successful in the early parts of the novel, the family's fortunes turn sour by the end, as Helene and Anatole meet untimely deaths. What is the significance of Tolstoy's representation of the sudden shift in the Kuragin fortunes?

5. At the beginning of the novel, Natasha is a bold, lively girl with a passion for life. By the end, however, Tolstoy emphasizes her stodginess—even dullness—and her careless disregard for her personal appearance. Is the final image of Natasha as a Russian matron a positive development, or a deterioration from her earlier liveliness?

# Review & Resources

## Quiz

1. With a discussion of what topic does Anna Pavlovna Scherer open the novel?

   A. Farming
   B. Money
   C. War
   D. Fashion

2. What is Vasili Kuragin interested in obtaining for his son Anatole?

   A. An officer's position
   B. A country estate
   C. A rich wife
   D. A law practice

3. Who is Helene's father?

   A. Count Rostov
   B. Vasili Kuragin
   C. Prince Bolkonski
   D. General Kutuzov

4. In what century is *War and Peace* set?

   A. The seventeenth
   B. The eighteenth
   C. The nineteenth
   D. The twentieth

5. What is Pierre's most noticeable physical feature?

   A. His large size
   B. His lameness
   C. His near-blindness
   D. His thinness

6. Who is the owner of the estate called Bald Hills?

    A. Pierre Bezukhov
    B. Count Rostov
    C. Vasili Kuragin
    D. Prince Bolkonski

7. Who is Mademoiselle Bourienne?

    A. Natasha's playmate
    B. Mary's companion
    C. Nicholas's first love
    D. Helene's rival

8. Who is severely wounded at the Battle of Austerlitz?

    A. Nicholas
    B. Andrew
    C. Pierre
    D. Kutuzov

9. Who is Pierre's first wife?

    A. Natasha
    B. Lise
    C. Sonya
    D. Helene

10. With which man is it rumored Pierre's wife is having an affair?

    A. Denisov
    B. Andrew
    C. Nicholas
    D. Dolokhov

11. What topic does the mysterious stranger Pierre encounters at the Torzhok station discuss?

    A. Spirituality
    B. Helene's misdeeds
    C. The war
    D. The devil

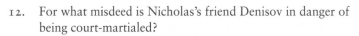

12. For what misdeed is Nicholas's friend Denisov in danger of being court-martialed?

   A. Seizing food supplies
   B. Insulting an officer's wife
   C. Falling asleep on duty
   D. Leaving the front without permission

13. How does Nicholas rescue Mary?

   A. He carries her out of her burning house
   B. He picks her up when she is lost in a snowstorm
   C. He calms the peasants who are rebelling at her estate
   D. He forces her out of the typhus clinic where she has been taken

14. What does Pierre madly and briefly imagine his mission in life to be?

   A. To denounce Helene
   B. To assassinate Napoleon
   C. To serve Napoleon
   D. To lead the Russian troops to victory

15. How does Helene attempt to marry another man while still wedded to Pierre?

   A. By bribing government officials
   B. By getting the tsar to denounce Pierre
   C. By killing Pierre
   D. By converting to Catholicism

16. Why do the Rostovs unload the carts containing their possessions during the evacuation of Moscow?

   A. To make room in their carts for wounded Russian soldiers
   B. Because the authorities forbid leaving the city
   C. To sell their belongings in Moscow at a high price
   D. To stay in Moscow and bravely face the French troops

REVIEW & RESOURCES

17. According to the narrator of *War and Peace*, which of the
    following best describes the Battle of Borodino?

    A. It is a French victory
    B. It prompts the signing of an armistice
    C. It is a Russian victory
    D. It is the site of Petya's death

18. In what public place does Natasha become interested
    in Anatole?

    A. The opera
    B. A church service
    C. A governor's ball
    D. A restaurant

19. For what does the dying Count Rostov beg forgiveness?

    A. Keeping a mistress
    B. Dissipating his family's inheritance
    C. Forcing Petya into the army
    D. Being cruel to Sonya

20. Who is Mary's brother?

    A. Pierre
    B. Denisov
    C. Anatole
    D. Andrew

21. What good deed ends up getting Pierre captured by
    the French?

    A. Saving a lieutenant from bandits
    B. Saving a child from a burning house
    C. Donating his cloak to a freezing old man
    D. Giving his bread to a French soldier

22. What causes Petya's death?

    A. A bullet
    B. The cold
    C. Starvation
    D. Illness

23. Through what Russian city, occupied by the French, does Pierre wander?

   A. Moscow
   B. St. Petersburg
   C. Smolensk
   D. Borodino

24. How does Platon Karataev die?

   A. He drowns in the Niemen River
   B. He is trampled by horses
   C. His amputated limb becomes infected
   D. He is shot by the French

25. What does Natasha do when Andrew rejects her?

   A. She burns his letters
   B. She becomes seriously ill
   C. She begs his sister to encourage him to reconsider
   D. She renews her acquaintance with Anatole

Answer Key:

1: C; 2: C; 3: B; 4: C; 5: A; 6: D; 7: B; 8: B; 9: D; 10: D;
11: A; 12: A; 13: C; 14: B; 15: D; 16: A; 17: C; 18: C; 19: B;
20: D; 21: B; 22: A; 23: A; 24: A; 25: B

## SUGGESTIONS FOR FURTHER READING

CRANKSHAW, EDWARD. *Tolstoy: the Making of a Novelist*. New York: Viking, 1974.

GUNN, ELIZABETH. *A Daring Coiffeur: Reflections on* WAR AND PEACE *and* ANNA KARENINA. London: Chatto and Windus, 1971.

MOONEY, HARRY J. *Tolstoy's Epic Vision: A Study of* WAR AND PEACE *and* ANNA KARENINA. Tulsa: University of Oklahoma Press, 1968.

MORSON, GARY SAUL. *Hidden in Plain View: Narrative and Creative Potentials in* WAR AND PEACE. Palo Alto, California: Stanford University Press, 1987.

SAMPSON, R.V. *Tolstoy: The Discovery of Peace*. London: Heinemann, 1973.

SANKOVITCH, NATASHA. *Creating and Recovering Experience: Repetition in Tolstoy*. Palo Alto, California: Stanford University Press, 1998.

SHIRER, WILLIAM L. *Love and Hatred: The Troubled Marriage of Leo and Sonya Tolstoy*. New York: Simon and Schuster, 1994.

TROYAT, HENRI. *Tolstoy*. Garden City, New York: Doubleday, 1967.

# SPARKNOTES
# TEST PREPARATION
# GUIDES

The SparkNotes team figured it was time to cut standardized tests down to size. We've studied the tests for you, so that SparkNotes test prep guides are:

### *Smarter:*
Packed with critical-thinking skills and test-
taking strategies that will improve your score.

### *Better:*
Fully up to date, covering all new features of the tests,
with study tips on every type of question.

### *Faster:*
Our books cover exactly what you need to
know for the test. No more, no less.

*SparkNotes Guide to the SAT & PSAT*
*SparkNotes Guide to the SAT & PSAT — Deluxe Internet Edition*
*SparkNotes Guide to the ACT*
*SparkNotes Guide to the ACT — Deluxe Internet Edition*
*SparkNotes Guide to the SAT II Writing*
*SparkNotes Guide to the SAT II U.S. History*
*SparkNotes Guide to the SAT II Math Ic*
*SparkNotes Guide to the SAT II Math IIc*
*SparkNotes Guide to the SAT II Biology*
*SparkNotes Guide to the SAT II Physics*

# SparkNotes Study Guides: